DIRTY
LOVE

EROTICA SHORT STORIES, VOL. 18

7 HOT STORIES IN 1
JUST PLAIN BOB

WARNING

This book contains sexually explicit scenes and adult language. It may be considered offensive to some readers. This book is for sale to adults ONLY.

Please store your files wisely where they cannot be accessed by underage readers.

* * * * * * * * * * * * * * * * * * *

About the Publisher

4Fun Publishing, a member of **BLVNP Incorporated**, 340 S. Lemon #6200, Walnut CA 91789, info@blvnp.com / legal@blvnp.com
NOTE: Due to the highly emotional reaction of some people to works of erotic fiction, any email sent to the above address that contains foul language or religious references is automatically deleted by our anti-spam software and will not be seen. All other communications are welcome.

DISCLAIMER

Please don't be stupid and kill yourself. This book is a work of FICTION. Do not try any new sexual practice that you find in this book. It is fiction and not to be confused with reality. Neither the author nor the publisher or its associates assume any responsibility for any loss, injury, death or legal consequences resulting from acting on the contents in this book. Every character in this book is over 18 years of age. The author's opinions are not to be construed as the opinions of the publisher. The material in this book is for entertainment purposes ONLY. Enjoy.

Erotica Short Stories, Vol. 18

Dirty Love

7 Hot Stories in 1

By: Just Plain Bob

© **Just Plain Bob 2015**
ISBN: 978-1-68030-343-8

My Di

Phone Sex

Doug's Toys

Chuck and Me

Melody Malone

Charlie Halloran

Gloria and Staci

My Di

The bookmakers in Vegas would have laughed at you if you have asked for odds on it happening or they would have just said, "Maybe a billion or a billion and a half to one." But happen it did and I'm sitting here at a table with my wife, watching as disaster walks straight towards me.

+++++++

Back in May, I received a phone call from a guy I used to work with. "You ready to leave Michigan yet?"

"Why? What's up?"

"The company I'm working for is looking for a few people with your qualifications. How does $3,800 a month to start sound?"

"About $900 a month more than I'm getting now."

"And that ain't all, bud: fully paid health insurance, nine paid holidays, one week vacation after a year, two after two and after five you get three. Throw in profit sharing and a company matching 401k, does it sound like something you might be interested in?"

"Who do I have to kill?"

"I'll send you an application. Send it back to me with a resume and I'll see if we can't get you out here to beautiful Colorado."

Three days later I received the application, sat down and filled it out then sent it back the next day. Ten days later I got a phone call inviting me to Denver for an interview. I flew out, was offered the job – which I accepted – then flew back home to break the news to my wife.

+++++++

Even after having been married for ten years I obviously didn't know Kirby well. I expected her to have a hissy fit at having to pack up and move twenty-four hundred miles to a city where she knew absolutely nobody, but all I got was, "Denver? That's a lot closer to South Dakota than here."

"What's in South Dakota?"

"That's where I was born and lived until I was seventeen and dad moved us here."

"You want to go back and visit I take it."

"I wouldn't mind going back to see Di again."

"Who is Di?"

"My best friend since kindergarten up to the eleventh grade; we kept in touch for about a year before I met you."

"What happened then?"

"I don't know. She just stopped answering my letters and when I tried to call her all I got was a, *this number is no longer in service*."

"Well, the good news is you will have plenty of time to go up to South Dakota and visit while I get to speed up on the new job. The bad news is you will have to stay behind and sell the house while I go on ahead. I'll start looking for a house as soon as I get there. With any luck our house is sold by then and I'll have a place for us to move into when you get there."

"When do you have to leave?"

"I have to be there on the eighteenth."

"Better stock up on vitamins and pep pills then."

"What for?"

"You are going to have to make love to me twice a day everyday until you leave to make sure that I have enough to hold me until I get there. Of course, you don't have to. I can always sample the local talent until you are ready for me.'"

"We better make that three times a day just to make sure that you can hold out."

"What's the matter lover, afraid some young stud might want to ring my chimes?"

"I know that some studs are going to want to. I just want to make sure that you don't give them the chance."

"Was there a compliment in there somewhere?"

"Come on, baby. I'll race you to the bedroom."

+++++++

The next couple of weeks were busy ones. I gave my two-week notice, bought a shell for the back of my pickup truck then started packing what I would need to set myself up in an apartment.

We put the house up for sale, did a survey of all we had to decide on whether or not we wanted to make the effort of moving it, and came up with quite a lot to put out in a garage sale. The night before I left, Kirby did her best to give me enough sex to hold me until we could be together again and in the morning I kissed her goodbye then headed for Colorado.

The trip took twenty-three hours of actual driving time and when I got to Denver I spent the first three days staying at my friend, Gene's house while I looked for a place of my own. I finally found an apartment that didn't require a long-term lease and moved in. Two days later I started my new job and then it was ten and twelve hour days as I worked at learning my new job and learning the ways of the company.

On my days off, I went house hunting. I was hampered by the fact that I had no down payment until my house in Michigan was sold so I ended up losing out on a couple of really nice ones. One day while I was looking at houses with a real estate agent, I commented on the fact that I was wasting the time of both of us and he asked why. I told him and he asked, "Can you come up with fifteen hundred?"

"Yeah, I can do that."

"That is all you need to get an FHA loan. You'll need to bring ten percent down at the closing, but fifteen hundred is all you need to get the ball rolling."

We went back to one of those that I liked and it was still available so I made an offer, it was accepted and then the owner asked me if I would like to rent the house while waiting for closing. The rent was only one fifty more than I was paying for my apartment so it was a no brainer for me. I moved in and set up housekeeping and that's when life got complicated for me.

+++++++

"You must have a house warming," Gene said.

"Yeah, but shouldn't I at least wait until Kirby gets here and we can get some furniture in the place?"

"Hell no, furniture will only clutter up the place. You got hardwood floors in the living and dining rooms and that's perfect for dancing."

"I still think I should wait for Kirby to move out here."

"You can have a real honest to god house warming when she gets here with invitations and everything. This one will be just for the people that you work with, just a little get together to get to know them better."

"Think so, huh?"

"Yeah, just some beer drinking, dancing, and socializing with the people you work with."

We set it up on a Tuesday after work and everyone came to my place instead of going to the bar for happy hour. No significant others, just the people from work.

I heard later that it was a pretty good party and the part of it that I remember was, but it got pretty drunk out for me and I have no idea what happened after I flaked out.

What I do remember is waking up in the morning with a hot mouth on my cock. I shook my head to clear it and saw Marie from Accounting looking up at me as her head bobbed up and down on my dick. Once she saw that I was awake she stopped sucking me, moved up and lowered herself onto my pole.

"I couldn't find an alarm clock to set for you so I decided to stick around and play alarm clock myself."

I had to admit that it did beat the hell out of hearing a 'click' followed by some radio station coming on, but it wasn't supposed to happen. I didn't cheat on Kirby. At least I never had before and I had never intended to, so how did this happen? It was too late to stop it. Actually, it had been too late when I woke up with my cock in Marie's mouth, so I just lay back and enjoyed it.

Marie bounced up and down on me for two or three minutes and then she said, "I can never get off when I'm on top. You awake enough to get the job done?"

"I can try," I said and I put my arms around her and rolled her over onto her back.

Another two minutes and she gave a little cry, her body shook a little and seconds later, I loosened my load. After a few seconds for her to catch her breath she said, "I'd like to do it again. Think you can get it up quick enough to do the deed and still get us to work on time?"

I did and we made it work with minutes to spare.

On the drive to work Marie asked, "When is your wife going to be here?"

"Not until we sell the house in Michigan, why?"

"Just want to know how long I have you to play with. We are going to do this again, right?"

"I don't really think that's a good idea. What happened this morning shouldn't have and I'm pretty sure had I been awake it wouldn't have."

"Don't be silly sweetie, if you didn't want it to happen there wouldn't have been a second time. For that matter, I'm only five feet one and soaking wet. I don't weight more than a hundred and ten pounds. You could have easily pushed me away when you woke up. What I am offering, sweetie, is a *no strings* attached all you can handle sex until your wife gets here."

"Why do you want to do that?"

"Because fucking other women's husbands is what turns me on and it is safe."

"What do you mean by safe?"

"No emotional involvement for one thing. Also, hubbies don't usually play around that much because they don't want to take anything unwelcome to the little woman. That means they don't give me anything either. Best of all, they usually don't tell."

"You make a good case, but I love my wife and I want to stay faithful to her. Well, as faithful as I can after this morning. I'm just not a fool around kind of guy."

"I know that about you sweetie, that is the reason I want you. You are exactly the type of married man I like. You love your wife so you don't play around and that makes you safe. Think about it, sweetie. Think about that slow, sensuous blowjob and the two times we played. You liked it and you can have all you want until your wife gets here and then I'll fade away."

+++++++

I'd like to say that I put her out of my mind and didn't give her proposition any thought, but I couldn't. Working ten feet from her ten hours a day, five days a week made that impossible. Whenever I looked at her I remembered that hot mouth on my cock and the tightness of her pussy as she rode me.

One of the things that help keep a married man faithful is that even though he might have an urge to play from time to time he doesn't have or want to spend the time and energy necessary to bed another woman. He doesn't want to make a play and be refused. He doesn't have or want to waste the time to date, to work up to the point where he tries the first kiss, the first tentative touching of a leg or breast, with the possibility of being turned down always lurking in the background.

I didn't have any of those obstacles facing me. Marie was there and she was ready. All I had to do was ask, "See you after work?" and it was a done deal. As far as the 'faithful' business was concerned technically I no longer was and Marie had been right. I could have easily pushed her away and I could damned sure have said no to the second round. Before the morning I found Marie in my bed I had gone six weeks without sex and it could be a month or two more before I could fly back and spend a weekend with Kirby or get her out to Denver.

I will say this – I tried. I fought it, I really did and I was successful right up to the night of Gene's birthday party. I wasn't drunk, but I did have too much to drink to drive safely and so I spent the night in Gene's spare bedroom. I woke up Saturday morning to a hand caressing my balls and a hot mouth on my cock and when I looked I was not surprised to see that it was Marie. She took her mouth off me and smiled, "Still playing at being an alarm clock although not to wake you up for work. Since we don't have to go to work today I wanted to wake you up early so we would have more time to fuck," and she went back to sucking my cock. I gave up the fight and we fucked three times before we got out of bed.

As we dressed she said, "You need to take me out to breakfast. I plan on fucking you all day and I need to store up some energy. I'll fuck you all night too if you can handle it."

Gene had the coffee on when Marie and I walked into the kitchen. He grinned at us and said, "I should have known better than to doubt her."

"What does that mean?"

"I told her not to waste her time on you, that you were Mr. Straight Arrow. I guess I never should have doubted her when she said she would get you."

"Hell Gene, you know telling me that is the same thing as waving a red flag at a bull. You know that will just make me try harder."

"You're right, I know. Go my children and fornicate in peace."

+++++++

Once I surrendered to Marie and we might as well have been husband and wife. We were together every minute that we weren't at work and when we were together we were fucking. Marie was a unique experience in that she had no hang-ups when it came to sexual gratification. If it turned you on, she would do it. She laid it all out for me one night early in our relationship.

"You want me on a picnic table in the park in broad daylight? I'm game if you are. Want me to suck you off in a movie theatre? I'll do it, but I get to pick the movie. Want to pee on me? Want me to pee on you? No problem sweetie, but if we do it at my place it has to be in the bathtub. You name it, sweetie, and I'm up for it. My goal is to completely satisfy you, and I do mean completely, until your wife gets here."

I wasn't into anything except the "Big Three" – oral, anal and vaginal – but Marie made damned sure that I knew that everything else was available. When it came to the "Big Three," she had no preference. Her biggest turn on, apart from fucking the husband of another woman, was from the situations where the acts took place. She loved being fucked on her desk at work when no one else was around and even though we both had beds that we could have gone to she did like to be taken on the seat of my truck in parking lots.

But Marie's biggest turn on was the one that made me feel the most guilty when we did it. She loved to be slowly ridding my cock or sucking it when I made my nightly call to Kirby. She never tried to make me moan or squirm or did anything that might make Kirby wonder about what was going on, but as soon as I hung up the phone Marie would be all over me like white on rice and the orgasms she had were tremendous.

And don't think for one minute that I didn't wonder about what might be going on, on the other end of that phone line. I had the utmost trust in Kirby, but then Kirby had the utmost trust in me and look what happened. All I could do was hope that if Kirby was playing, it was with Marie's male counterpart – someone in it just for the sex – and I fervently prayed that I would never know about it and that Kirby would never know about Marie.

+++++++

On one of the rare nights that Marie didn't have my cock in one of her orifices I sat in a bar having a drink with Gene. The subject of Marie and me eventually came up and Gene laughed and said, "When it's over bud, is when you will find out that it really isn't over."

"What the hell does that mean?"

"Marie is honest when she says that when your wife shows up your affair will be over and she will move on, but what I'll bet that she hasn't told you is that fucking other women's husbands isn't all there is to her jones."

"You need to explain that to me."

"She gets off on talking to the wife."

He saw the alarm come over my face and he laughed, "No, she doesn't rub it in. It just turns her on to sit across from the wife and make general conversation while thinking to herself, 'I fucked your husband.' She has even become good friends with some of them. She won't shoot you through the grease, but you could do yourself in by the way you act around Marie when she's with your wife."

"That's how it usually happens. She will see the two of you together and she will walk up to you and say, 'Is this your wife? Introduce me.' You don't want to be nervous and give off vibes that your wife might pick up on."

"Oh great! Just fucking great! That's me all right, Mr. Stoneface. Hell Gene, I had to quit playing poker because everyone could read my face like an open book. Kirby would know in a heartbeat."

"Then best you make sure that the two of them never meet."

+++++++

Two weeks after my conversation with Gene we had an offer on the house and we accepted. I flew back for the closing, rented a U-Haul truck and loaded up everything and headed back for Denver, but not before Kirby spent three days trying to fuck me to death. She was going to wait a week and then fly out. The drive back to Denver in the under-powered U-Haul took almost four days and when I got back Marie was waiting for me.

"Hurry up, lover," she said as she peeled off her clothes, "I have to get as much as I can before she gets here."

We fucked up a storm for the next three days and on the morning of the day that Kirby was due to fly in, Marie gave me one stupendous blowjob and then got to work sanitizing the house so that no trace of her remained. Then she gave me one last passionate kiss, told me goodbye and I left for the airport.

+++++++

After we settled in and Kirby had spent a month trying to catch up on the sex she had missed she asked me if it would be alright if she took a few days to visit family and friends in South Dakota. I of course said it was okay and to take as much time as she needed. She called me the next day and told me that aside from seeing two aunts it had been a wasted trip.

"Nobody I knew stuck around. As soon as they could they all took off for bigger cities."

"Didn't find your old girlfriend I take it?"

"No, near as I could find out Di left town just about the time I lost touch with her. I'm going to get a good night's sleep and head on back tomorrow. I should be home before you go to bed. If not I'll try not to wake you."

"You can wake me if you want to."

"Oh? Would you like that? I know just how to do that."

I knew what she meant of course and it made me suddenly feel guilty as hell when I remembered that Marie used to wake me the same way.

The thing I had been dreading most – Marie meeting Kirby – became moot when Marie was promoted and transferred to our Houston office. The next six months flew by. Kirby found a job that she liked, I was doing well at my job and the redecorating of our house was coming along and all in all I was pretty content.

The holiday season snuck up on us and then it was time for the company Christmas party. Kirby and I were sitting at a table with Gene and his current girlfriend when all of a sudden Kirby squealed, "Oh my God, I don't believe it. I just don't believe it. It can't be, but it is."

"Don't believe what, sweetheart?"

"She's here! My Di is here!"

"What are you talking about?"

"My girlfriend, the one I've been trying to get in touch with is here. There she is, over by the door, that's Di, that's my Diane Marie!"

I looked over at the door and a cold hand grabbed my heart. Marie stood there surveying the room, saw me, smiled and headed straight for our table.

End of the 1st Story

Phone Sex

I wanted to scream at her. Actually, killing her would be too nice a way to end the torture. Day after day she continued to drive me nuts and there wasn't anything that I could do about it. I couldn't take the problem to management because all that would do was made me the laughing stock of the office. The problem? Working in a cubicle next to a woman who couldn't be made to understand that cubicles are not sound proof and that I could hear every word she said – every fucking word! Why was that so bad? Because she had phone sex with her husband two or three times a day.

It had been going on for almost a month. For three months the cubicle next to mine had been empty and then one day I saw Jerry, our maintenance man, moving a desk into it. I asked him what was up and he told me that the company had hired a new engineer, "And I hear that she is one hot mama."

That was borne out the next day when a drop-dead gorgeous redhead started carrying boxes into the cubicle. I introduced myself and offered to help her move her stuff in. It took me two trips to her car before I noticed the wedding ring on her left hand. Just my luck, I was going to be sitting next to a stone fox all day, everyday and she was spoken for. Her name was Belinda and she had just graduated from M.I.T and was excited about starting her new job. 'Enjoy the excitement while you can, honey,' I thought, 'They will grind you down soon enough.' The bosses at our office might not be as bad as the 'pointy-haired' boss in the Dilbert cartoon, but most of them are pretty damned close.

The first week she was there went so-so. The food in the cafeteria sucks so I asked Belinda to lunch a couple of times and we exchanged vitals – me, single and not looking and she – married and no kids. Our hobbies were somewhat similar: skin diving in the summer and skiing in the winter. Other miscellaneous stuff – I hated TV with a passion and only used it for watching football. She on the other hand was a slave to *The King of Queens*, *Friends*, *Dharma and Gregg* and two soap operas that she taped while she was at work.

I suppose that the only reason that I asked her to lunch was that she was so damned easy to look at. It was during the start of the second week that everything started to go bad.

+++++++

It was a Tuesday morning and I heard the phone ring in Belinda's cube. She answered it and the conversation went something like this:

"Oh hi, glad you called. I missed kissing you goodbye this morning. Oh yeah baby, I would have kissed that too. Where are you? Can anyone see you? Take it out for me, baby. Got it out? Stroke it for me, baby. Slide your hand back and forth and think of my pussy lips, wet and puffy and waiting for you to slide it in me. Think of how hot I am sitting here and thinking about what that beautiful piece of meat could be doing to me right now. Oh you bet, lover. The crotch of my panties is soaking wet. What? Don't be silly, baby. You know what my favorite number is where you are concerned. Yeah, you got it baby, sixty-nine. Hey, got to go. Keep stroking it baby, I want it ready for me when I get home. Love you to, bye."

The first time I thought it was kinky and I envied the guy she was married to, but by Wednesday I had a totally different take on it. She had conversations with him at lunch and again at three on Thursday and on Friday it was at nine-fifteen, eleven-thirty and two forty-five. If she was homely or barely good looking I probably could have tolerated it, if only for the humor involved. But Belinda was not ugly, homely, plain looking or in any other way a dog. To listen to her talk about sucking cock, eating pussy, making love and yes, even taking it in the ass while I sat there visualizing her doing those things was killing me. Thursday was more of the same, but it was Friday that destroyed me and ruined my entire weekend. Her phone rang at nine-fifteen:

Hello? Oh hi, baby. Thinking of me? Ooh, how naughty. Don't be silly. No. I just wish it was Christmas because there would be mistletoe and I would have ran around kissing guys under it. Do you think they would notice the taste of your cum? I know baby, I can be so wicked at times. You must have shot a quart in my mouth this morning. It's too bad I don't have a boyfriend on the side here at work so I could kiss him and let him taste you. No silly, I wouldn't tell him. Would you like that? Would it turn you on to know that I was kissing a guy after you had cum in my mouth? I'll do it, baby. I'll do some flirting here – some heavy necking – and let some guy slip his tongue into my cum-soaked mouth. You bet. Just tell me when baby and I'll do it. Love you too baby, see you tonight."

I had sweat on my upper lip and it was all I could do to keep from running over to her cubicle and shouting, "Me, pick me!"

+++++++

My weekend sucked! No matter where I went, no matter what I did I had a head full of images of Belinda catching me under the mistletoe. What really made it bad was that Christmas was only two weeks away and every fucking store I went to was decorated for the holidays and that kept the thought of Belinda alive in my mind.

Monday started off bad. By eight-thirty she was on the phone telling him how horny she still was, "I know you did me twice this morning baby, but it wasn't enough. Me too, baby. I wish there is a motel or hotel close so we can meet for lunch. Yeah baby, I know. I won't get any work done today thinking about it. Okay lover, keep it hard for me. Love you, bye."

There was more of the same at eleven and three-thirty and I ended up going to the men's room and beating my meat. Tuesday, Wednesday, and Thursday were more of the same. I wasn't getting my work done, I was missing deadlines and I was a wreck when I went home. Friday was the absolute worst, but I couldn't complain much about it because I did most of it to myself. The phone rang at eleven-twenty and Belinda answered it:

"Hello? Oh hi, lover. Yes. Yes. Of course I'm thinking of you. You bet. Got the Polaroid in my desk drawer. (a giggle) I'm looking at the one where you have your beautiful cock buried in my ass. What? Oh god no, I loved it. It did hurt to start with, but it felt real good in the end. (giggle) I made a pun didn't I? Of course you can. Yes, as soon as I get home. Just have the KY ready, baby."

Five minutes later she asked me if I wanted to go to lunch with her, but I begged off – I told her I had some errands to run.

As soon as she was gone I hurried into her cube and looked for the photos. I found them in an envelope in the bottom right drawer and as I looked at them my cock almost ripped through my pants. There were eight all together, one each of her with a cock in her mouth, ass and pussy, two of her fucking herself with a dildo, and three naked poses for the camera. I made a quick trip to the copy machine and made myself two copies of each picture – one for the office and one for home – and then I returned the originals to where I had found them. At three-forty as I listened to her tell her husband what she planned on doing to him over the weekend I looked at the photos and wished that cubicles had doors so I could beat myself off. I took the photos home with me and over the weekend I wore my poor cock out.

The next week was Christmas and the holiday came on a Friday. When I got to work on Monday, Belinda was already there and she was decorating her cube with ornaments and a small plastic tree. Then she built an arch over the entrance to her cubicle, wrapped it with garland and put a sprig of mistletoe right in the center. I wondered what she would do if I went over there and kissed her under it. That day was as bad as any of the others had been, but the morning call was the worst:

"Hello? Oh hi, lover. I had a great weekend, but I can hardly sit in my chair. What? I know, I know, but maybe we overdid it. Maybe we should leave my ass alone on Sundays. No baby, no. Honest, I loved it and I want to do it again – soon! What? Tell you what. Why don't you meet me for lunch and I'll give you a blowjob in the car. You know how much I love the taste of your cum. Okay baby, see you then. I love you too, bye."

The entire time she was having her conversation I was looking at the photos and wishing I could haul out my cock and jack off. At lunchtime I asked her if she would like to have lunch with me just to see what she would say.

"Sorry, I can't. I have to meet my husband over lunch and take care of a personal problem. Maybe we can do it tomorrow."

The three o'clock call was the killer:

"Hello? Hi babe. Yes, I can still taste it. You must have had a quart saved up. What? What if I'm wearing nothing but heels and hose when you get home? No. No. I don't care how much I wore the poor thing out over the weekend. I bet I can still get it up tonight. Okay.

Want to bet? Okay, if I can get you up I get to have my ass fucked, if not I have to go to bed hungry. (Laugh) Of course I loaded the bet my way. What did you expect from your cock crazy wife? Okay. Love you too, see you tonight."

I spent another night with the Polaroids in one hand and my cock in the other.

+++++++

Tuesday, Belinda was already at work when I got there. I settled in and tried to get some work done before the distraction of the morning phone call. At nine-thirty the phone rang:

"Hello. Good morning you big cocked stud. Of course I do. Yes. Yes. I know baby, I know. I'm sitting here with your cum leaking out of my pussy. What? Baby, I'm so wet that it will probably soak through my panties, my skirt and stain the chair. (giggle) No, that doesn't count the load you put in my mouth just before I left."

While Belinda was talking I opened my desk drawer to get out my copy of her photos and I froze. There, on the photo of her with a cock in her ass, was a lipstick imprint and underneath were the words, *I'll give you the originals if you want them.*

In her cube Belinda was saying, "Don't you wish I could be swapping tongues with someone right now? Would that turn you on? Just imagine my cum-coated tongue sliding into another man's mouth. Do you think it would make your dick hard, baby?"

I lost it! I got up, left my cube and went over to Belinda's. She heard me coming and she turned in her chair. I pulled the sprig of mistletoe off her little arch and put it on my head and then I took the phone out of her hand and said into it, "Hang on, she'll be back in a minute." I set the phone down on her desk and then I kissed her. I forced my tongue into her mouth and I held her until she responded and let her tongue wrestle with mine and then I broke the kiss. I picked the phone back up, "She won't be lying to you," and I gave Belinda back her phone and went back to my desk.

I heard when she said, "Is your dick hard, baby? Can you picture him with his tongue in my cum-soaked mouth? Good baby, keep thinking about it and your dick will be nice and hard for me when I get home. What? (giggle) Maybe I'll bring you a surprise. See you tonight. Love you too."

I heard her hang up and a minute later she came into my cubicle. "Took you long enough. I was afraid I was going to have to come over here and spread myself on your desk. Is your cock hard?" and she bent over and touched the lump in my pants. "Ooh, that's good. Would you like a blowjob at lunch baby, or would you rather fuck me? You have a van, right? I want to take my hubby a surprise tonight."

She took hubby a couple of surprises that night. We both got dirty looks from our supervisor when we came back late from lunch, but it's hard to get two fucks and a blowjob out of the way in under an hour. While resting between bouts she told me the story. Her husband had a thing about her fucking another guy and she had finally agreed to give it a try if she could find someone that she liked enough to do it with. She'd found a couple, but they had turned out to be obnoxious assholes so she had taken a pass on them. When I had helped her move into the cube next to mine she thought that I could possibly be the one. When I hadn't made any moves by the end of the first week she had hit on the idea of the phone calls to entice me. She wasn't going to be the one to make the first move. She would have felt like too much of a slut if she had made the approach. She hadn't expected me to be able to hold out for more than a few days, but I had surprised her. The longer I held out the more determined she was that I would be the one to fulfill her husband's fantasy. She was getting desperate. She wanted to give him his fantasy as a Christmas present, but I wasn't cooperating. The photos (they were a plant for me to find), the arch with the mistletoe, and the phone calls were all a desperation attempts to get me to make a move. Happily for me, they worked.

I've not met her husband, but we have settled into a curious relationship. He sends Belinda to me every morning freshly fucked and I eat her pussy at lunch, get a blowjob and then I make a sperm deposit and send her back to him. According to Belinda he eats her pussy as soon as she gets home so I guess he is as big a cream pie junkie as I am.

Every other Friday after work Belinda and I check into a motel and she is very late getting home to her hubby, but she does go home to him full of what he wants. She says she wants to do the same for me – she will fuck him all night and come to see me on a Saturday or a

Sunday. I told her to go ahead and set it up. Belinda says her husband is hinting at wanting to watch, "How do you feel about having him in the closet watching? I'm not going to tell him that I told you he'd be there, but I wouldn't feel right about doing it if you didn't know."

"I get to do everything? Including something that you haven't let me do yet – your ass?"

She laughed, "Why? You think you'll get your jollies listening to me grunt like a pig while you do it?"

I grinned at her, "No, but if I'm going to do that for him I want to get everything that he gets."

It was her turn to grin, "Next Monday work for you?"

End of the 2nd Story

Doug's Toys

She looked at herself in the mirror and shook her head. 'What a waste,' she thought. This much to offer a man and it was going to waste, but not for much longer.

Doug and Martha had gone steady during the last two years of high school, had become engaged the day after graduation and had married one year after that. The first five years had been very good and then, slowly, things had gotten ho-hum and common place, at least as far as Martha was concerned. He had a good job and made good money and Martha, since finding out that the two of them couldn't have kids, had also gotten a job. Between the two of them they made enough money to have the things they wanted. For Martha it was the house, good furniture, and a new car every three years. For Doug it was toys – lots of toys – and that was the problem.

Doug's sex drive seemed to be inversely proportional to the number of toys he acquired. The more toys he had, the more time he spent with them and the less time he spent with Martha. It might have been different if Martha was included when he played with his toys, but all too often she was excluded in favor of "the boys." It was another truism that the more toys Doug got the more buddies he found who wanted to spend time with him.

"I can't take you with me, honey. You would be the only woman there and I know these guys. I'd turn my back on them for a minute and they would be hitting on you. I can't expose my wife to behavior like that."

'I wouldn't mind Martha thought,' at least someone would be paying me some attention.

One week it would be dirt bike racing and the next Doug and his buddies would take the boat out to the lake for a weekend of fishing. Hunting season meant four weekends of taking the ATV's and going out looking for deer. Then there was the week Doug took off to go elk hunting, and the weekends devoted to duck, quail, pheasant, and dove hunting. Besides hunting and fishing there were the two nights a week that Doug bowled. The Friday night card games and on the weekends when he was not off somewhere killing things, he played golf on Saturday and Sunday. That left Tuesday and Wednesday for Doug to devote to Martha and half the time on those two nights he was just too tired. Well Martha was tired too – tired of being ignored.

Martha knew that it had nothing to do with her looks. She still turned heads and got hit on quite a lot and not just by Doug's buddies. She wondered how long they would stay buddies if Doug knew how many of them had tried to fuck her. No, there were plenty of other men who wanted her. There were a good half dozen or so where she worked who had let her know they were interested. Several times she had stopped after work to socialize with the people she worked with and she had danced with some of the men. A couple of times when she'd had a few too many, she had engaged in some necking and she could even have gone farther if she had wanted to. Other girls she worked with had made trips out to the parking lot or to the motel next door and she could have done it if she had wanted. Even though her body craved for a man's touch she had behaved because she loved Doug, but she was rapidly reaching the point where that wasn't going to be enough to keep her honest.

The final straw came one night after she had stopped with her coworkers for drinks after work. She had just enough to loosen her up and she had let herself get seriously felt up on the dance floor. She had even gone out to the parking lot with the man, necked with him for quite a while and had even let him get a finger in her pussy. It was only when the man had taken out his cock that she had panicked, pushed him away and hurried home. She was hot, she was horny and she needed Doug to make love to her. When she got home he was in the basement tying flies and getting ready for his next fishing trip with his buddies. She tried to get him to go upstairs and make love to her, but he ignored her and concentrated on his fly tying.

"Not now Martha, I need to get another dozen of these done."

She had gone upstairs in tears and as she threw herself down on the bed she vowed that there would be some major changes made and that they would be made real soon.

+++++++

Doug came home from work to find Martha sitting at the kitchen table looking over some papers. He bent and kissed her on the forehead, "Hi babe, whatcha doing?"

"Just reviewing some financial stuff."

"Yeah? What kind of financial stuff?"

"Just reviewing our net worth."

"Why?"

"Just curious."

"We in good shape?"

"Depends on how you look at it."

"What's that mean?"

"Sit down and I'll show you."

Doug sat down and Martha handed him a sheet of paper. "This is our net worth."

Doug scanned the sheet of paper, "Not bad babe, not bad at all. We're doing alright for ourselves."

Martha handed him another sheet of paper and Doug said, "What's this one?"

"That's what it looks like after the divorce."

"What? What the hell are you talking about? What divorce?"

"The one that's just around the corner if you don't make some changes around here."

"What are you talking about, what changes?"

"I'm tired of playing second fiddle to dirt bikes, ATV's, fishing boats and fishing trips. I'm sick and tired of taking a backseat when it comes to bowling, golf, hunting, poker parties and anything else you and your buddies decide to do. In short – you had better make some room in your life for me or I am going to rearrange your life. This is a community property state and it is also a no-fault state. If I go for a divorce everything we have gets sold and we split the proceeds fifty-fifty and your toys will be gone and so will I. You need to decide whether you want half the pot or to spend some time with me. I'm young, I'm healthy and I want a love life. I'm tired of lying on the bed and looking at the ceiling while you tie flies or some other bullshit thing like that. So, you either take care of your husbandly duties or I either get a divorce or start having affairs. I am not I repeat not going to go without anymore. The next time I want to make love in the morning and you push me away and tell me, "Sorry babe, but I'm playing golf this morning," the next time I walked naked into the basement and you tell me to go away and let you tie flies or the next time you chose your buddies or your toys over me I will break it off in your ass."

Doug sat there speechless and stared at Martha as she stood up and left the room.

+++++++

There were a couple of days of frosty silence after Martha's little speech and then things began to get better. Doug paid a lot more attention to Martha and soon they were back to making love almost as often as when they had first gotten married. Doug still played with his toys and spent time with his buddies, but Martha did seem to have first call on his attentions. For six months things went along fine and Martha wondered why she hadn't put her foot down sooner. Then Doug went and got drunk and things changed.

It happened during a weekend fishing trip with some of his buddies. One of his buddies brought along a girl he had picked up in a bar. Everybody got drunk and the girl had pulled a train for the guys. Everyone nailed her at least three times and Doug woke up the next morning with a hell of a hangover and the knowledge that he had fucked up big time. He knew he had to find some way not to have sex with Martha until he was sure that the girl he had just helped gangbanged hadn't given him a disease. For the next three weeks he made excuse after excuse to Martha as to why he couldn't make love to her. The excuse was plausible, he said he had hurt his back at work and he walked and acted as if he had, but that didn't keep Martha from being frustrated.

The Friday night poker game was when it all came unglued. Martha was in the basement folding laundry when two of Doug's buddies went into the downstairs bathroom. Because of the way the heating ducts ran Martha heard every word the two men said.

"Martha seems to be a little upset with Doug tonight."

"Think she found out that he fucked that skank that you picked up?"

"I don't know. I don't think so. If she knew about that gangbang

I think she would be a lot more pissed than she seems."

"Speaking of gangbangs, I'd sure like to nail Martha sometime."

"We all would. We've tried to get Doug to bring her along on the fishing trips, but he won't do it."

"I think he knows what we would do if we got the chance."

"I think she'd go for it if we got enough booze in her."

"Wishful thinking guy, wishful thinking."

Martha stood there looking down at the folded laundry in front of her. Doug could gangbang some fucking whore, but he couldn't fuck her? Her mind went into overdrive as she plotted her revenge.

+++++++

The following Tuesday, Martha stopped after work with some of the people she worked with. She danced with several of the men and didn't protest when they thought they were sneaking a feel. It was when she danced with Kevin that things started to happen. As he held her close his erection was pressing into her leg.

"My goodness, is that for me?"

"It is if you want it."

"Oh I want it, I most definitely want it."

It was Martha's first time in a backseat since high school. As Kevin's cock filled her pussy she wondered how many other men she should let have her before letting Doug know. Kevin's cock felt good in her and she thought she could learn to like having backseat affairs. Martha liked it so much that when Kevin came in her she sucked his cock to get him up again and then she let him have her a second time. The next night she stopped for drinks and gave herself to Kevin again. The next day at work Mark had stopped by her desk, "Are you and your husband splitting up?"

"Why do you want to know?"

"Just curious. If you are breaking up with your husband and Kevin is your new boyfriend that's one thing, but if you are just out having fun, I want you to know that I'm interested and I'd love to play too."

That night at the bar, Mark was the one who made the trip out into the parking lot with her and later, when Mark and Kevin had gotten in an argument over her she had stopped it with a simple, "You two stop that. I've got enough for the both of you," and then she had gone out into the parking lot with them and proved it.

Two more weeks went by and during that time Martha had let every man she worked with who wanted her take her out to the parking lot. One night she had lain on Kevin's backseat while four men had taken turns on her for almost two hours. She had gone home that night to find Doug waiting for her.

"Good news, babe. My back is better and I think I might be able to take care of you tonight."

Martha's mean streak surfaced and she smiled sweetly at Doug, "I just might consider it if you eat my pussy."

"Lead the way to the bedroom babe, I'm ready."

She lay there staring up at the ceiling as her husband sucked the combined juices of four men out of her and wished it could have been more – she wished she had so much in her that it would drown Doug.

"Christ babe, you sure are wet."

"I know, sweetie. I've been hot and horny for so long that it just built up in me."

When Doug sank his cock in her she thought, "That's it you bastard. You like gangbangs so much that you shouldn't mind that you are number five tonight."

+++++++

For the next month Martha fucked the men she worked with and then went home to Doug. She insisted that he ate her pussy before he fucked her and she was amazed that Doug never caught on to the fact that he was sucking up cum and getting sloppy seconds. But as much as Martha was enjoying what she was doing to Doug she still wasn't satisfied. She wanted to do something that would really rub his face in it. She wanted to do something that he would know about. She wanted to do it right in front of him. She wanted to do something that would show him just how she felt about his betrayal. Martha knew what she wanted to do, but she just had to wait for the right time and the right set of circumstances. And then Doug gave her the opportunity that she needed. "Can you do me a favor, babe?"

"I don't know. What is it?"

"We have a rush order that has to go out tonight and I'll be a little late in getting home. The boys will be here for poker at seven. So, could you take care of things until I get home?"

"Take care of things?"

"Yeah, you know, seeing that they get chips and dip, beer and whatever they want."

"Whatever they want? Yeah, I think I can do that."

"Thanks babe, I'll owe you one."

By seven-ten the game was in progress. Martha started them out with beer and chips and then she went into the bedroom and took off her dress. She had already taken off her panties and bra. She put on a garter belt and rolled nylons on her long legs and then she stepped into a pair of five-inch heels. She checked herself out in the mirror and smiled to herself, 'Nobody going to turn you down tonight girl,' she thought as she turned and headed back to the game. The room went silent when she walked in. She looked around at the six gaping men and smiled at them.

"A little birdie told me that all you guys want to fuck me. He said that you want Doug to bring me on a fishing trip so you could liquor me up and then gangbang me, is that right? Well, we don't need no liquor or a fishing trip to get that done now, do we? You want me here on the table or in the bedroom?"

All six had fucked her once and she had a cock in her ass and one in her mouth when she saw Doug walk into the room. She took her mouth off the cock she was sucking, "Dougie, you're home. Oh goody, come join the party."

"What the fuck is going on here?"

"It's a gangbang, sweetie. You know all about gangbangs right? That's what this is all about, sweetie. I'm just trying to find out if I am a better fuck than that barfly you gangbanged on your last fishing trip. How about it guys? Am I better? Would you like me to join in your fishing and hunting trips from now on?"

Martha looked around the room and saw that all the guys were looking nervously at Doug.

"Hey, don't be looking at him. I'm the one with the hot, hungry pussy and I'm a long way from wanting to quit. She leaned forward and recaptured the cock she had been sucking and went back to work on it.

Several seconds later the cock in her ass began moving again and out of the corner of her eye she saw that not one of the guys was making a move to get dressed. It looked like Doug was in for a long hard night and she was glad because it meant that she was too.

End of the 3rd Story

Chuck and Me

It was a difficult situation. On the one hand I owed the man my life and on the other the same man had just ruined my life and I wanted to kill him. Oh God did I ever want to kill him.

+++++++

I'd known Chuck damned near all my life. We grew up three houses from each other on Delancy Street. We went to school together, dated the same girls and played on the same teams. We were closer than brothers. He'd had my back and I had his many a time and everyone knew that if you fucked with Chuck you were fucking with me and if you fucked with me you got Chuck in the bargain.

If Chuck dated a girl and he scored he would tell me and I would try my hand with her. If I took one out and hit a home run, I would tell him and he would ask her out. We shared a lot of girls that way.

But grade school and high school relationships sometimes come to an end and it happened with Chuck and me. After graduation I followed my old man into the foundry, but Chuck wanted something different than the hot hard work in the foundry and he joined the Army.

+++++++

I saved my money until I had enough to get myself an apartment and then I started out on my own. I dated some, scored some, but never did find a girl who gave me that special tingle. I never found one until I met Merrily. It was at the company Christmas party and the only reason I was there was because that was where they handed out the Christmas bonus checks. My plan was to show up for the free feed, listen to the inevitable rah-rah speeches, get my bonus check and then leave to go check out some of the really jumping parties that I knew would be going on.

I saw her sitting at a table with one of the recently hired

draftsmen. From the looks of him I thought that she would probably be his daughter and not her husband or date. She wasn't a raving beauty, but something about her kept drawing my attention. I was looking at her when she turned her head and her eyes met mine and she smiled. I'd always heard about smiles that would light up a room, but I'd never seen one until then. All thoughts of leaving the party went out the window and when the band set up and played its first number I got up and went over to her and asked her if she would dance with me. She said she would be delighted and when she stood up I almost said:

"Oh my God."

You couldn't see it when she was sitting down, but she had a killer body and she was a tall girl. I'm six two and her nose was level with my chin. Of course the fact that she was wearing four-inch heels helped put her there. Those heels told me something about her. They told me that she was one confident woman. Most tall girls won't wear a four or five-inch heel because they feel it intimidates guys to have a girl as tall as them. Merrily's shoes said:

"Here I am! Are you man enough?"

I've never been a shy one and as soon as I took her in my arms and introduced myself I asked:

"Are you married?"

"No."

"Engaged?"

"No."

"Going steady?"

"No."

"Any guys around that you are hanging up with and are hoping that they can ask you out?"

"No, none of the above at this time."

"Then please allow me to apply for any or all of the above."

"Well, I might consider you for the last one, at least for starters."

"In that case I must do what is expected of the man who holds that position. Will you have dinner with me tomorrow?"

"I would love to."

And so began my relationship with Merrily Ashton Martin. It was not a smooth road, at least not from my perspective. I wasn't the only guy who liked tall, confident women. Her "Are you man enough" attitude made quite a few guys step up to show that they were, but I was persistent and I hung in there and eventually Merrily and I became a couple.

At the next company Christmas party I danced her over to be under the mistletoe, kissed her and then went to my knees and proposed. I don't know whether she was more surprised or embarrassed, but when I handed her the little velvet-covered box she opened it, took out the ring and handed it to me and offered me her left hand so I could slip the ring onto her finger. When I stood up she put her arms around me and gave me a passionate kiss as everyone in the place hollered, yelled and applauded. We were married in a civil ceremony the first week of June.

+++++++

Merrily was a secretary in the home office of a large insurance company and we decided to bank her paycheck until we had enough for a down payment on a house. My apartment was larger than hers so she gave up her apartment and when her security deposit was returned it went into the down payment savings account. When I got my Christmas bonus at the end of the year it gave us enough and we found a nice three bedroom that was equidistant from her office and the foundry.

Life was good. I liked married life. I enjoyed waking up in the morning snuggled up to Merrily. I couldn't wait to get home to her when I got off work. When I was home I wanted to be with her – close enough to touch – no matter what she was doing. Merrily owned me!

I wasn't stupid. I knew that regardless of how I felt about her and how she felt about me (and it certainly seemed to me that she felt about me like I felt about her) my "hovering" would eventually get on her nerves. She needed some personal space. I told her she needed to get out of the house, have some personal time, at least one night a week. She said that the same held for me and we decided that each of us would take one night a week as a 'night out.' That actually gave each of us two nights away from each other. I took mine on Thursdays and bowled and Merrily took whatever night the girls she worked with decided to get together for dinner and drinks.

We talked about kids, but we both decided to wait a while before taking on that responsibility. We would wait until after we had been some places and done some of the things we wanted to do.

+++++++

Merrily and I had been married just short of three years when one night the phone rang and Merrily answered it.

"Honey, it's for you. Some guy named Chuck."

Chuck had been discharged and was back in town. He wanted to know if I could meet him at Riley's Tavern to suck down a few beers and catch up on what had gone on since he left town.

"The major thing that happened is that I'm now a married man."

"It goes without saying that she is invited too, only fair since I'll be there with my bride."

On the way to Riley's I explained to Merrily who Chuck was and what our history was. Chuck was sitting in a booth in the back with an absolutely ravishing redhead. He rose to meet us and after a double bear hug with lots of back slapping I introduced him to Merrily and he introduced us to his wife Rita.

We drank beers and talked about where he had been and what he had done and I brought him up to date on what was going on with our old classmates and friends. I asked him what his plans were and he told me that he was home to stay.

"I talked to Ferguson this afternoon and I start at the foundry on Monday."

It was getting late so we set a date to have dinner on Saturday and maybe go to Grady's Road House for some drinks and dancing. As we were driving home I asked Merrily what she thought of Chuck and she hesitated just enough so that I noticed before she said:

"He seems real nice. I like him."

"Him not they?"

She hesitated again before saying, "I didn't like her."

"Any particular reason?"

"Just a feeling."

"A feeling? What kind of a feeling?"

"She's just a little too full of herself. Didn't you notice how she was constantly checking out the guys in the place to see if she had their attention? How she constantly moved in her chair to show a little more leg to the guys who were looking at her? I'm betting the marriage won't last and I'm betting that other men will be the reason for the break up."

"Is this some of the famous "woman's intuition" that I've heard about?"

"Laugh if you want to baby, but believe me when I say that girls know about things like this."

We had dinner with Chuck and Rita on Saturday and then went out for drinks and dancing. Regardless of her misgivings about Rita, Merrily and Rita seemed to get along fine. In the coming months, and not surprising given my friendship with Chuck, the four of us spent a lot of time together. Chuck and Rita had an apartment and curiously enough it was the same apartment that Merrily and I had lived in. I don't mean the same apartment complex, but the same exact apartment. Talk about weird! Anyway, because their apartment wasn't really big enough to entertain in they spent a lot of time at our house. We would play cards, have barbecues and stuff like that. Merrily and Rita never did get really tight, but they were friendly enough to each other even to the point that they went out on a couple of 'girl's nights out' together.

+++++++

Chuck had been back about six months and the four of us were at the Starlight Lounge one Saturday night and I was dancing with Rita. I was into the music, had my eyes closed and was grooving when I heard Rita whisper in my ear:

"I want it. When can I have it?"

"When can you have what?"

"Your cock, lover. It wants me and I want it."

That was when I became aware that I had an erection and that Rita was rubbing her leg against it. I quickly pulled back from her and she giggled and said:

"Not to worry, lover. She has her back to us and my hubby is clueless as always."

Just then the music ended and I pulled away from Rita and led her back to our table. We were only there for another hour and I never asked Rita to dance again, but every time I looked in her direction she was looking at me and as soon as she saw me looking at her she would give me a small smile and lick her lips. I wrote it off as too much to drink and/or a joke in poor taste. I didn't mention it to Merrily.

It was two weeks later on a Sunday and Chuck and Rita were over for a barbecue. We had been drinking beer and shooting the bull for about an hour and I got up to go use the bathroom. I took my whiz, shook off the last few drops and washed my hands. I unlocked the door and opened it to leave and found Rita standing there. She walked straight to me so I had to step back and when we were both in the bathroom Rita pushed the door closed and locked it.

"What are you doing, Rita?"

"Shush baby, we don't have that much time. It would have helped if you hadn't already tucked it away."

She went to her knees in front of me and I tried to step back but the sink was behind me. Rita's hands went to my zipper as she said:

"You know you want this, baby. Hurry up, let Rita see whatcha got."

She had my zipper halfway down before I could stop her and I admit that looking down at that gorgeous face on a level with and only inches away from my cock gave me an erection. She saw the tent form and giggled then said:

"I knew you wanted me, lover."

By then she had my cock out and she leaned forward and licked the head as I was saying:

"Stop this, Rita. It isn't right and you know it."

"Bullshit lover. And don't give me the 'I can't do this to my best friend' shit. If we weren't here he would have your honey bent over the picnic table and be doing her doggie."

I put my hands on my shoulders and said, "You are crazy, Rita," as I pushed her back and she sat down on her ass on the floor. I moved around her and got the hell out of the bathroom.

It was another hour before they left and as we walked them to the door and gave the little "goodbye hugs" that friends exchange. Rita whispered in my ear:

"I'm going to get you lover, and soon."

After they were gone I grabbed another beer and chugged it down and Merrily said:

"What's wrong? You seem uptight about something."

I told her what had happened in the bathroom and then I told her about what had happened at the dance.

"I'm not surprised," she said, "I told you that I had a feeling about her. One of the reasons I stopped going on 'girl's nights out' with her was that she kept disappearing out into the parking lot with guys she danced with. I never followed her to see what she was doing, but I had my suspicions that it was more than just a little necking. You going to tell Chuck?"

"God no! He loves her. She is all he talks about at break times and during lunch. He either wouldn't believe me or if he listened to me, checked up on her and found out it was true he would hate me for being the one to tell him. Either way it would kill our friendship. It's a no win situation for me. I'll just have to keep my distance from her or make sure that there is someone else around when I'm near her."

"Well honey, if she is doing it with you, she will be doing it with others. Hopefully he will find out about her from someone else."

A couple of months went by and although we went out with Chuck and Rita every two weeks or so and had them over for cards and barbecues I never let Rita get me alone. She was always watching me and when I would look her way if no one else was looking she would wink at me, lick her lips or blow me a kiss.

+++++++

Chuck had been back for almost a year when he saved my life. I was standing on the foundry floor reviewing some figures on a clipboard when I heard someone yell out, "Look out, Rob!" and then something hit me hard and I went flying and ended up lying on the floor. I heard a loud crash and I rolled over and looked and saw a pile of steel ingots on the floor where I had been standing.

"You okay?"

I looked over and saw Chuck on the floor with me. I shook my head yes and asked what happened. The overhead crane had been moving a pallet of steel ingots from the yard to Furnace 3 when one of the cables on the pallet sling let go. The pallet started to tip towards the corner of the pallet that the broken sling had been holding and Chuck saw it. He threw himself at me as the ingots started sliding off the pallet.

I looked at the pile of ingots and knew that if Chuck hadn't managed to get me out of the way they would have been cleaning me off the floor with a sponge.

"I guess I owe you a beer."

"Or three," he said as he stood up and then offered me his hand to help me up.

The two of us got rip-roaring drunk that night and I had to call Merrily to come and get us since we could barely walk, let alone drive.

A month or so after the accident I was offered a foreman's position. It was on swing shift which meant that I would be working three to eleven-thirty. With Merrily working days and me working swings the only time we would see each other would be on the weekends. The upside was that Mike Taylor, the day shift foreman, would be retiring in a year and then I could move to day shift. I talked it over with Merrily and while neither of us was too keen on the idea of only seeing each other on weekends, Merrily pointed out that the increased pay would put us in a financial position where we could finally think about having kids. We decided that I should take the job.

I'd been on swings just a little over nine months when one Tuesday at 11:45 AM the phone rang. It was Chuck. He was in jail and he wanted to know if I could come down and bail him out. I rushed down and got him out and found out what had happened. He had beaten a guy so bad that the guy had to be taken to the emergency room at the hospital.

Our company had a random drug testing program. At any given time they could come up to you, tap you on the shoulder and tell you that your name had just come up. You left work, went to the clinic, peed in the bottle and then went back to work. The next day the results would be back and if you tested clean life went on. If your test was positive you were out of a job. Chuck had been picked that day and when he left the clinic he decided to stop by the apartment for a "quickie" with Rita. The problem was that when he got to the apartment he found that in order to have that "quickie" he would have to wait in line until the guy fucking Rita was done. While he was beating the snot out of the guy Rita was on the phone calling 911.

I took him home with me and told him he could bunk in the spare bedroom, that I did not want him going back to his apartment that day. I was afraid of what he might do to Rita that might put him back in jail. Chuck said that he didn't think she would be there as he had told her while the cops were cuffing him that she would be next when he got home. I called Mike Taylor and let him know why Chuck wasn't back on the job and then I called Merrily and brought her up to date on the situation.

Chuck stayed with us for two days and then he went back to the apartment. Rita had cleared out and had taken everything of value with her when she left. Nobody heard from her again. Chuck couldn't even find her to serve her with divorce papers. He was pretty broken up over it as he really did love Rita. He spent a lot of weekends with me and Merrily just for the company as he tried to get over it.

+++++++

Three months sailed by, Mike Taylor retired and I was getting ready to move to day shift. I was really looking forward to being able to spend more time with Merrily. The year of swing shift had been hard on us.

I remember it as clear as crystal. It was the Saturday before I was to move to day shift. It was eleven-ten when Merrily came into the kitchen and sat down at the table across from me. I put the morning paper down and she looked at me in silence for several seconds and then she said:

"I'm pregnant."

"Honey, that's wonderful," I said as I stood up to go around the table to hug her. She put out a hand to stop me and said:

"No it isn't. Unless my diaphragm failed it isn't yours."

"What? What are you saying? What do you mean it isn't mine?"

"I'm sorry Rob, but unless the diaphragm didn't do its job the baby is Chuck's."

Stunned, I sat back down on my chair and stared at her. She couldn't meet my eyes. She looked down at the table and the story spilled out of her. She had gone off her birth control pills three months ago, but she wanted to plan her pregnancy so the baby would arrive in late May or early June so she used a diaphragm on the weekends we made love and also on the occasional nights she waited up for me to come home. The rest of the time it sat in its case in the medicine cabinet and that was where it was on the night that Chuck stopped by.

He had been drinking and he was a mess. He was going through a particularly bad time and didn't want to be alone. He and Merrily had sat and talked and then he had started crying and sobbing, "How could she do that to me? I loved her so much. Why did she do it?" and on and on. Merrily went over and sat by him and took him in her arms and tried to comfort him. She held him tight while he cried himself out.

"I don't know how it happened, Rob. I honestly don't know. I remember kissing him on the forehead and saying something like, "There, there, you will get over this," and then we were making love on the couch. He came in me and then broke down again over betraying you.

"He was sobbing and crying and I felt sick over what had just happened. I couldn't change that it had, but I could try to get him to calm down so I hugged him and told him that it would be alright, that you would understand. That was a mistake. He was still in me and while I was hugging him and trying to get him to stop crying he got hard again. I tried to push him away, but he started moaning, "Goddamn you Rita, how could you," and he was driving hard into me and I just wasn't strong enough to push him off.

"When it was over he begged me to forgive him and told me that he would wait with me until you got home, confess and tell you that none of it was my fault. I knew what it would do to you and your friendship and so I talked him out of it and told him that since it would never happen again it would be best to just let it be our little secret. And it would have been except for what he left in me. I had to tell you now. I couldn't wait nine months and pray that the baby wouldn't have Chuck's red hair."

I just sat there with tears in my eyes and stared at her. The silence stretched out and finally Merrily said:

"Say something, Rob. For god's sake say something."

I couldn't speak. I had tears running down my cheeks as I got up and walked out of the house.

My mind was a blank for the next several hours. It was 4:45 in the afternoon and I was sitting in my car at Hawkins Point and looking out over the lake with no idea how I got there. I was still sitting there when the sun came up the next morning. I felt like everything I had worth living for had been ripped from me and stomped into the mud. I felt empty inside.

I drove to the nearest ATM and withdrew the maximum amount allowable and then I took off down the highway. I drove for days until my money started to run low. I stopped in a town in Ohio and sold my car to a used car dealer and then walked into a recruiting office and joined the Army.

I'll finish my basic training at Ft. Leonard Wood next week and only God and the Green Machine know where I'll go next.

I haven't called home to let anyone know where I am. What would be the point? I can never go back. I know for certain that if I did and were to see Chuck I would do him serious – extremely serious bodily harm and I'm not at all sure that I wouldn't kill him. And the way I'm looking at it the Army and wherever they send me has to be better than prison.

And Merrily? I could not bear looking at her as her belly swells with the constant reminder of her betrayal with the man who used to be my best friend

End of the 4th Story

Melody Malone

I was in Los Angeles on business and one day I was in Century City for a business conference and when we broke for lunch I headed for a restaurant I'd heard about. I was walking down the street when something slammed into my shoulder and I heard a voice say:

"Watch where you're going asshole."

I turned and saw a guy standing there looking at me and smiling. It took me about half a second to recognize Bill Gibson and I stepped to him and took him in a big bear hug. Bill and I had grown up together and had been friends since fourth grade. I'd lost track of him when he dropped out of college in our junior year. We had exchanged cards and phone calls for a while and then life got in the way and I hadn't seen or heard from him in almost ten years.

He asked what I was doing in LA and I told him I was on a lunch break and he practically dragged me to a small bar that served sandwiches and we settled in to play catch up on each other's lives. I filled him in on my marriage and divorce and what I was doing for a living and he told me about his two marriages and two divorces. I asked him what he did for a living and he told me he was a film producer.

"No kidding? What are some of your films?"

"I doubt that you have seen or heard of any of them. They have been mostly low budget independent films."

"I've seen some of that kind of stuff. Give me a couple of titles."

"Well, one of my biggest was *Diary of a Sex Crazed Housewife*."

I sat there stunned when I heard that. He saw the look on my face and said, "What?"

"That was yours? You produced "Diary?" The one starring Melody Malone?"

"Yeah, that one and a ton of others like it."

"I can't believe it. My old buddy is a king pin in the porn industry."

Bill looked at his watch and said, "I've got to run, but I'm having a party at my house tonight. You have to come." He gave me directions and I told him I'd be there and he took off.

+++++++

I couldn't believe that Bill was a porn film producer. Of course he probably found it hard to believe that I knew some of his films well enough to know who starred in them. I owed that to my ex-wife. In our third year of marriage she decided that our sex life needed spicing up so she started stopping at an adult book store on her way home from work and rented tapes to bring home.

They did spice things up, but unfortunately they also made Claudia curious. She saw all the big cocks hanging from the porn stars and she started wondering what a big one (mine measured in at 6 ½ inches) would be like. Too bad for her because on one of the days she was finding out I came home early from a working lunch with a mild case of food poisoning.

But Claudia had me hooked on porn videos. Not because they spiced up our sex life, but because it turned out that one of the porn stars was an old girlfriend of mine.

I'd met Mary when we were both enrolled in Business Law III during our senior year. I asked her out and we dated several times and then things got hot and heavy between us and I was about to propose when her father died. She flew home to be with her family and never came back. I tried several times to get in touch with her, but I never saw her or spoke to her again until Claudia brought home *The Playful Housewife*.

I don't think Claudia ever had a clue as to why I fucked her seven times that night. Oh she knew it was because of the video, but she never knew that while I was fucking her I was thinking of Mary and what she had been doing in that video. Mary sucked Peter North's cock and as I watched I remembered how great she had been at giving me head. When Mary took Sean Michaels's cock up her butt I remembered how tight it had been when I spent time there and seeing her on tape in threesomes and more blew my mind.

After tossing Claudia out on her ass I started hunting adult bookstores and video arcades looking for porn starring Mary and I had nineteen of them on the shelf next to the VCR. I'd watch one and think of what I had lost when I hadn't gotten off my dead ass and flown back to her home town instead of leaving phone messages.

+++++++

Bill's party was already cranking along when I got there. He handed me a beer and then introduced me to a bunch of people, some of whom I recognized from the porn videos that I watched.

"You still like to play poker?" Bill asked.

"Have a standing game every Friday night when I'm home."

"Good. There's an open seat at the table," and he led me over to a table where a game of seven-card stud was in progress. Bill introduced me, warned them that I was no stranger to the game and then took off to look to his other guests.

I'd been playing about an hour and I was doing okay. I was a winner, but not a big winner and that was okay because I never am. I play for the enjoyment of the game, the challenge of trying to read the other players, of bluffing to win and to not let myself be bluffed.

I was sitting there looking at my hand and trying to read the other players. The game was a five-card draw. I had opened for twenty and gone into the draw with a pair of kings and had drawn three cards, two nines and a jack of clubs. There were three besides me still in the hand. Two had drawn three cards, which indicated they had gone in with a pair, and the third guy had drawn one card. Since it was jacks or better to open and he had passed to begin with I knew that he had tried to draw to a straight or a flush. Whether or not he had hit I would know if he called or raised. The question was how high a pair had the other two drawn to and had they gotten any help.

While I was sitting there trying to work things out in my mind an arm reached over my shoulder and picked up my empty beer bottle and placed a full one down in its place. I mumbled distracted thanks and then bet twenty bucks. The guy on my left called, the next guy threw in his cards indicating that he hadn't filled his straight or flush. The third guy raised me ten, I called and the guy to my left folded. The third guy laid down his kings and sevens and said, "Shit!" when I put down my kings and nines.

The next hand was my deal and I called a five-card stud. After the deal I had a deuce looking up at me. I checked my hole card and saw another deuce. The guy to my left had a jack up and he bet ten. Everyone called and I dealt the next card, nobody paired visibly and I gave myself a six. The jack was still high and he bet another ten and everybody called. I dealt the cards and gave myself another deuce. That gave me the only visible pair, which made me high. With three of a kind I felt pretty strong, but a large bet would probably drive at least two or maybe even three of the other players out of the hand.

Conventional wisdom was to bet and drive them out before they could get help. But the more that stayed in the larger the pot. With one card remaining to be dealt and no other pair showing I felt I could gamble – that was what we all sat down to do, right? So I bet ten and everyone stayed.

The last card gave everyone a pair showing, but the six of spades that I dropped in front of me gave me two pair showing. I had the high hand and so I bet twenty. The man to my left had paired his jack and he raised me twenty which meant that his hole card paired one of his other up cards, but not the jack or he would have been betting before that. The next two dropped out. The next guy called which told me he could beat two pair jacks high. He had a pair of sevens showing but he only called because he was hoping he wasn't going against three jacks. The last guy tossed in his hand and I called the raise and kicked it another twenty and everyone folded except the jacks to my left. He called me and then smiled at me when he turned over the third jack. He had done just what I had done; he kept the bet low to enlarge the pot. The smile slipped a little when I turned over the third deuce and showed him my full house.

As I raked in the pot one of the guys said:

"He's won two pots in a row with you standing behind him Mel. How about sharing some of that luck with the rest of us?"

I turned and saw Melody Malone standing behind me.

"Sorry guys, but he is a stranger in a strange town and I've appointed myself his guardian angel."

She smiled at me, reached down and picked up my beer and drained it and then took the empty and walked away. She was back in a couple of minutes with a full one and she set it down in front of me and then she wandered away. I lost the next five hands and then she came back and stood behind me and watched the game. I won the next three hands and then she wandered away again and I lost the next two. I told the guys to deal me out and I started to stand up and one of the guys said:

"Oh sure, just come in here, win all our money and then leave."

He was joking and I knew it, but I also knew that I shouldn't come into Bill's house and leave a bad taste in the mouths of his friends so I counted out what I had won – almost six hundred – and I tossed it in the middle of the table.

"Six hundred boys, match it and I cut you high card for it."

"You're kidding. All six of us draw against you?"

"High card takes it all," I said.

The six guys put up another six hundred and one of them shuffled the cards, offered me the cut and when I shook my head no he spread them out across the center of the table. I told them to draw first and while they were pulling out their cards Melody came up to me with a fresh beer and then stood there watching. The six were all smiles as they laid down their kings, queens, jacks and tens, but the smiles all faded when I pulled my card and turned it over. It was the ace of hearts.

"Thank you gentlemen, it has been a most interesting evening and I hope we can do it again sometime."

As I was picking up the money Melody wandered off again. I was walking away from the poker table when Bill came up to me.

"You going to let me in on your little secret?"

"What secret is that?"

"What have you got that has this city's hottest porn star hanging over your shoulder?"

"I'm sure that it had nothing to do with me."

"Bullshit old buddy. Mel has been to dozens of my parties and she has never – I say again with emphasis, NEVER – gone over and stood by the poker table. And she has never – one more time with even more emphasis, NEVER – gone and got a guy a beer. She did it three times for you."

"I don't know, Bill. She said something about me being a stranger in a strange town. Maybe it is because I'm the only one here that she doesn't know."

"Uh-huh. You're holding out on me pal, but I will find out," and he walked away.

I spotted Melody Malone talking to three other women I recognized from my video collection and then I went out onto Bill's deck for some fresh air. I'd been there five minutes trying to see stars through all of LA's light and haze when I sensed someone behind me. I turned and there she was.

"Hello Mary."

"It's Melody now or Mel for short. How are you, Bob?"

"Fine, yourself?"

"I'm good. I don't mind telling you that it was a major surprise to see you here."

"No more of a surprise than my seeing you."

"Forgive my nosiness, but why are you here?"

"Bill and I grew up together. I was in town and he invited me over."

I saw what I took to be disappointment register on her face and I jokingly said:

"What? You thought that I had finally tracked you down?"

She looked me straight in the eye and said, "A girl can always hope."

I stared at her in silence for several seconds and then said, "If that was your hope, why did you never return my calls? Why did you not make some effort to keep in touch with me? Why did you just disappear on me?"

"It is a long story, Bob, and not a pretty one, but I can't talk about it here. Would you follow me home if I asked you to?"

"No."

Again I saw disappointment and I hastened to add, "Give me directions and I'll come by, but Bill is already curious about why you spent so much time around me tonight. I don't know the situation or relationships here and I'd just as soon keep a low profile until I know more. You leave and I'll wait half an hour and then I'll come by or I'll leave and you wait the half hour."

"You ashamed to be seen with the nasty porn whore?"

"No, I'm just looking out for you. Not having the slightest idea about your life so I'm trying to prevent talk that might cause you problems."

"That's sweet of you, but these are my friends and they all know me well enough that nothing I do surprises them. They will be curious and eventually one or two of them will ask about you and I'll tell them the truth."

"And just what is the truth?"

"At my place, Bob. Let's get out of here."

Mary was hanging on my arm when I went to say goodnight to Bill and tell him I was leaving.

"Still going to tell me there is no secret?"

"There are secrets, bud and then there are secrets."

"That doesn't make sense to me."

"Some secrets are shared, bud. I can't tell you what Mel might not want you to know. The secret is hers to tell not mine."

"I'll tell you later, Bill," Mary said, "But not now. I'll call you in a couple of days. Right now I'm going to take Bob home with me and fuck his eyes out."

My eyebrows went up at that and Bill's jaw dropped, but before any more could be said Mary tugged on my arm and led me away.

+++++++

I don't rent cars when I'm in LA. It is a whole easier to use cabs and let someone else be the frustrated driver dealing with the road rage so I squeezed myself into Mary's little BMW convertible for the ride to her place. I tried to start up a conversation, but she shut me down with:

"Not until we get to my place, Bobby. I'll tell it all tonight, but my way and to my schedule."

"Schedule?"

"You'll see, Bobby. It won't be long now, just a few more minutes."

We pulled up to a gated community and the security guard at the gate tipped his hat and said, "Good evening Ms. Malone," as he opened the gate for her. She pulled in a driveway, used a remote to open her garage door and we pulled inside and parked. The entry door from the garage led into the kitchen and as we walked in Mary said:

"Do you remember the last time we made love?"

I did and I told her so.

"It was on the kitchen table in that little studio apartment you had. That's where I want to pick things up."

I turned to her and saw that she had already let her dress slip to the floor and she was standing by the kitchen table kicking away her thong. She sat on the edge of the table and spread her legs.

"I want to pick up where we left off, baby. I told Bill I was going to fuck your eyes out. That is the schedule I mentioned. I'm going to fuck you until you can't walk or see straight and then we can talk."

There she sat on the edge of the table, the girl who had fucked my brains out in college, the woman whose videos I had memorized and who I had cursed myself for letting her get away and I was going to say no? As I dropped my trousers to the floor I wondered how many back home would ever believe me if I told them that I had fucked one of the most well-known porn stars in LA on her kitchen table.

I knew she expected me to step up to her and drive my cock into her, but I didn't. I lowered my face to her clean shaven pussy. Touching it only with my tongue I kicked her little button as she squirmed and pushed her pussy at me. I pulled my face back and just kept on licking. She was panting and moaning and I pushed a finger into her cunt and was rewarded with an, "oooohh godddd." I pushed another one in with the first and she screamed and bucked her hips up at me and I latched onto her clit with my lips and sucked it for all I was worth and she exploded in what I hoped was one of the best orgasms of her life.

I stood up and put my hard cock at the entrance to her pussy and hesitated while mentally chanting to myself, "Wait for it, wait for it," and then it came:

"Do it, do it damn you, do it! Don't tease me, just do it!"

I shoved my cock forward and she was so hot and wet that I slid right in. I lifted her legs up onto my shoulders and began pushing into her with long hard strokes as she lay there on the table thrashing and screaming at me to fuck her and make her cum. I fucked her as hard and fast as I could until, with a long drawn out moan, she came. I felt the walls of her cunt trying to clasp my cock and I felt her hot juices flowing around my cock head and I exploded into her.

I stood there, her high heels next to my ears, looking down at her. I felt something flutter around my shrinking cock as her pussy tried to hold onto it and damned if it didn't start to come back to life. She felt it too and she said:

"The couch Bobby, the living room couch. This table is too hard on my back."

I picked her up and carried her into the living room and set her down on the couch. By then I was hard enough and I pushed her legs apart and thrust into her. She responded and I slowly started to fuck her pussy. I pushed in deep, slowly withdrew, held still for a fraction of a second and then pushed deep again.

"No," she cried out in frustration, "Don't tease me Bobby, fuck me. Fuck me hard."

I ignored her. This wasn't going to be just another fuck session, at least not for me. I had no idea if I would ever get to do this again so I was going to do it my way.

"Damn you, Bobby. Fuck me," she cried and tried to buck her hips up at me in an attempt to get herself off, but I pulled back out of her until she held still and moaned:

"Oh please, Bobby. Please god, don't do this to me. Fuck me Bobby, please fuck me," and then I slid my cock back into her.

I did it several times and each time as I sensed her orgasm approaching I stopped and waited several seconds before I began again. She was begging me to let her cum, but I kept toying with her until I felt myself ready and then I fucked her fast and furious. "Oh fuck!" she screamed as she came and at the same time I blew my load deep into her. She held me to her as my cock went limp and then she said:

"My bedroom Bobby, take me to my bedroom. It's at the top of the stairs."

I picked her up and carried her up to a room with a king sized bed. I set her down on it and she pulled me down with her. She kissed me long and lovingly as her hand fondled my cock. She sent her tongue probing into my mouth and I sucked on it until she broke the kiss and moved down to take my cock in her mouth. I knew she was wasting her time. Hell, I'd just cum twice in the space of twenty-five minutes. It would be an hour before Mr. Happy would be ready to play again. Mary proved me wrong. It took her ten minutes, but she got me iron bar hard again.

"This time I want you in my ass," she said as she got on her hands and knees. "You know I'm not a virgin back there Bobby, but go slow until you get all the way in."

I slid my cock in her pussy to get a coating of our juices on it and then I slowly pushed myself into her tight little ass. She hissed out a low, "Oh yes, oh God yes," and started pushing her ass back to meet my strokes. She moaned with pleasure as I plowed her butt with long hard strokes. I reached under her and my fingers found her love button and I rubbed it. Her entire body shook with the strength of her orgasm and as she was coming down from it I shot my cum up inside her.

I fell to the bed and she lay down and rolled up against me and we kissed. She pulled me out of the bed, led me to the bathroom and washed off my cock. Then she went down on her knees and went to work trying to get me up again. It was the most exhausting night of my life.

+++++++

I lay next to her on the bed, breathing hard and wondering why she couldn't accept it as a lost cause as she fondled me in a vain attempt to get me up one more time. Finally I said:

"Okay Mary, you win. My eyes are still in my head, but I seriously doubt that if I got out of bed I could walk."

"I keep telling you it is Melody now, or Mel, but not Mary."

"You can be Melody or Mel to your adoring fans, but you are always going to be Mary to me. Now, the first half of your schedule is out of the way so how about telling me why you ran out on me. Why didn't you come back from your father's funeral?"

"He was my step dad and I didn't go to the asshole's funeral. I just used his death as a way to get away from you and don't take that wrong, Bobby. Before you say a word let me explain. You were getting ready to ask me to marry you and I had to get away from you before that could happen."

I started to say something, but she put a finger to my lips and said:

"Hush baby, let me get it all out and then you can talk. I loved you Bobby and I would have loved being your wife, but I would have been a lousy wife and you would have ended up hating me. I considered marrying you and then tried to keep my bad side hidden, but I knew I would eventually get caught or someone would tell you about me."

"Tell me what?"

"That I was a cock hungry slut, that I was a round-heeled whore. That under the right circumstances I was anybody's fuck toy."

She saw the look on my face and said, "It's true, Bobby. I've been a slut since my step dad took my cherry at a very early age. Even when I was dating you I was fucking other guys and I would have kept it up even after we got married. I love sex Bobby, lots and lots of sex. Have you seen any of my videos?"

I nodded a yes.

"I'm not an actress, Bobby. What you see when you watch my videos is the real me. I'm not acting. I'm doing what I love to do. I knew that about myself Bobby and I couldn't do it to you, I just couldn't. But I did love you and I would have said yes if you had asked me to marry you. I would have done it and it would have ruined your life so I ran."

"How could you be so sure it would have ruined my life?"

"You would have come home early one day and found me with someone or someone who knew us both would have seen me going into a motel or hotel and would have told you. In fact I'm surprised that no one ever told you about what I was doing while we were dating, about all the backseat time I had or the frat parties where I pulled trains."

"Did you ever stop to think that I might have loved you enough to share – to let you be yourself as long as you were mine?"

"No baby, I didn't. But it doesn't matter because you know you wouldn't have."

"How can you be so sure?"

"Because you threw your wife out on her ass when you caught her doing what I most likely would have been doing."

"How in the hell did you know that?"

"We have mutual acquaintances and I talk with them from time to time and I always ask about you."

"No one ever mentioned that."

"I asked them not to baby, I didn't want to open old wounds to no purpose. I almost walked out of Bill's tonight as soon as I saw you, but I couldn't."

"Why couldn't you?"

"Because I've missed you, Bobby. You are the only man I've

ever loved enough to consider marrying. Once I decided to stay it was all I could do to keep from throwing myself at you and jumping in your lap."

"Why didn't you?"

"Because I was afraid you would push me away and tell me to leave you alone."

"Well I didn't, so what now?"

"What do you mean?"

"Do I just get up, get dressed, say thanks for the trip down memory lane and leave?"

"That's about the way I had it figured. The only difference is that I was going to try and keep you company for as long as you are out here. How much time is that?"

"Four more days. I'm scheduled to fly out of LAX on Friday afternoon, but I could change it to the Sunday night red-eye. Six days isn't even close to the lifetime I wanted, but I suppose it is better than nothing at all."

"I can promise you a fun filled six days if you would like."

"How are you on weekend visits?"

"You would fly out here just to see me?"

"Or fly you to Denver. If you'll remember, Colorado is lovely this time of the year."

"I remember, but it isn't a good idea."

"Why not?"

"Out here no one thinks twice about seeing someone in the porn industry. Being seen with a porn actress on your arm in Denver would create quite a buzz."

"I'm a big kid and I think I could handle it. Besides, think of the reputation it would give me with the local ladies. They would flock to me just to see what it was that had a famous porn star keeping company with me."

"Don't joke about it, Bobby. Something like that could hurt you as far as your reputation in the business world went."

"Sorry, but now that we've connected I don't want to not see you again. I'll transfer out here. We can pick up where we left off. I'm talking marriage here, Mary."

"Don't be stupid, Bobby. It couldn't work now for the same

reason that it wouldn't have worked back then. I wouldn't change. I wouldn't stop being me. I still would want lots of sex and not to hurt your ego baby, but you can't give me enough to keep me home. Look at you right now. I'm playing with your cock trying to get it up again and it is just lying there. You said it yourself, your eyes are still in, but you don't think you could get out of bed and walk. On the other hand I'm ready for more. I want more. If there was another guy here, or two or three for that matter, I'd jump out of this bed and leave you here while I fucked them."

"Maybe I could handle it. Did you ever think of that? And don't throw Claudia up at me. She was Claudia and not you."

"It doesn't matter, Bobby. Even if you could live with being a cuckold I couldn't live with you being one. I would end up losing all respect for you if you could just sit back and let me be a whore. I'd come to see you as a wimp and I'd bring guys home with me and do it in front of you. I'd ask you to eat my pussy after they came in me. They would make fun of you and the word would get out that you were a wimpy cuckold and people who know you would laugh at you, behind your back at first and then eventually to your face. No Bobby, I won't do that to either of us. But now that we are back in touch I do want to keep seeing you. Maybe once a month you can come out here for a weekend."

"What's the difference if I come out to see you or stay here with you?"

"I can be true for a weekend Bobby, maybe even for as long as a week, but after a week all bets would be off. Let's take what we can work with, Bobby."

"I guess I don't have much choice then, do I?"

+++++++

I spent the rest of the week with Mary, but when Friday came I went right from my meeting to LAX and caught my flight home. I didn't tell Mary. I left for my meeting that morning with her expecting me back and expecting me to stay until late Sunday. I couldn't do it. I'd spent years regretting that I hadn't gone after her when she left for the funeral and then I found out that it wouldn't have mattered if I had.

The memory I had of Mary was a false one. Still, I would have loved to stay with her, but I knew in my heart she was right and that I couldn't live the life she had predicted for me.

When I got home the nineteen videos I had of Melody went into the trash since there was no sense watching them and eating my heart out for something that I now knew could never have been.

In the weeks following my return from LA Mary left several messages on my answering machine, but I never returned the calls. I received three letters and I returned them unopened. I got home from work one night and found four phone calls from Bill on my machine. I called him and after some small talk he asked me what I had done to Melody.

"Nothing, why?"

"All she's done since you left is mope around."

"I don't know what the problem is, Bill. All I did is get out of her life."

"Why in god's name would you do a thing like that?"

"Because she painted me a picture of the living hell my life would be if I stayed in hers."

"Well boss, you know where to find me if you ever come back to LA. Don't be a stranger now, okay?"

"Sure enough bud, I'll look you up. I still need to give your buddies a chance to win some of their money back."

+++++++

Thirty minutes after I hung up the phone my doorbell rang and I opened it to find Mary standing there with a suitcase.

"I've been sitting in a motel for the last six hours waiting for Bill to call me and tell me you were home. May I come in?"

I stepped aside to let her in and I closed the door and turned to see her standing there looking at me.

"I've taken a personal vow of fidelity Bobby, to you and only you. I don't know if I can do it, but I do know that I have to try. I have to do what I didn't do ten years ago. I have to give us a chance. Will you let me, Bobby? Will you let me try?"

I stepped forward, took her in my arms and kissed her and then I picked up her suitcase, "Let me show you around the place."

All I can do now is cross my fingers and hope.

End of the 5th Story

Charlie Halloran

I'm sure that you have heard the expression that "no bad deed goes unpunished" and I'm here to tell you that it is so very true.

Lana and I had been married for twenty years and she was the light of my life. She had only one fault as far as I was concerned – she was a cock teaser. She had a great body that she kept nice and tight with daily workouts in the home gym she had set up in our basement. At five two, one hundred pounds, and with a set of hooters that stretched the tape at 38 D, she was a walking wet dream and she knew it. She was proud of her tits and did several exercises that had no other purpose than to keep them firm. Her dresses and blouses were all low cut to show them to their best advantage, and show them she did, every chance she got.

One of her favorite pastimes was to go grocery shopping bra-less in a t-shirt and shorts and at least once a month she did what she called her "slut" walk. Shorts, t-shirt, bra-less and in her high heeled "come fuck me" pumps, she would spend an entire day at the local mall just strolling from store to store creating hard-ons. Me? I loved it because she would come all hot and bothered and try to fuck my brains out. Earlier I called her a cock tease, but that's not really true, at least not in the strictest sense of the term. She wasn't a mean tease, you know what I mean, the kind of girl who would French kiss you for an hour, squeezing your dick all the while, and go and leave you with a case of blue balls. No, Lana just liked to flaunt her tits, knowing all the time that she was generating erections. That isn't to say that guys didn't try to get in her pants, they did all the time, but to the best of my knowledge no one ever got close.

Life was good, my sexpot of a wife and I were happy together and then things started to go sour. I didn't detect it right away, but Lana's whole personality started to change. She went from happy-go-lucky to quiet and moody, but the change was gradual, not sudden. When it did finally dawn on me that things had changed I began looking for the cause, but I couldn't find anything that I could identify as the problem. One night after a fairly intense bout of lovemaking she asked me a question that I'd not heard from her in our entire marriage:

"Will you always love me, no matter what?"

I told her that of course I would.

"Promise? No matter what?" and again I assured her that I would.

+++++++

Annie, our married daughter, brought the grand kids over to visit and Lana didn't seem to enjoy having them around like she normally did and I made the comment to Annie that I hoped the kids wouldn't be too disappointed at granny being down in the dumps. And she said:

"Well, I expected it, with all that's going on. That's the real reason I brought them over today, to see if we couldn't cheer her up."

"What do you mean by all that's going on?" I asked.

She looked at me and I saw understanding cross her face, "She hasn't told you, has she?"

"Told me what?"

"No, no," Annie said, "I'm not going there. It's not my place. You have to get it from her."

I spent the rest of the day in a blue funk waiting for Annie and the kids to leave so I could confront Lana. Annie hadn't even cleared the driveway before I went to Lana and said:

"I want to know what's going on."

"I don't know what you mean," she said.

"Oh yes you do," I replied, "Annie almost told me, but then she said I had to get it from you. Come on, out with it."

Lana started crying and ran for the bedroom and I followed and got there before she could close the door on me. "I'm not going away. We will just sit here for as long as it takes for you to tell me what's going on."

It took me ten minutes before I got it out of her. She'd had her yearly exam and the doctors had found a lump in her right breast. After several tests they had told her that she was going to have a mastectomy – they were going to remove her right breast. Now, as a male, my attitude was, "So what? You are still the best looking woman in the world and you will still look better with one breast than a lot of women who will still have both," but as I said, that was the male talking. But Lana wasn't a male, she was female and she was totally devastated that one of those two perfect mounds of flesh that she was so proud of and that she'd had so much fun with was going to be taken from her. It did not matter what I said, or what anyone else said. No one would ever find her attractive again. Her life was over.

+++++++

She had the operation and then she withdrew into herself. I forced her to go to parties and social events, but she never had any fun at them. One night as she was getting dressed for a party that she did not really want to go to she said:

"I don't know why you insist on taking me to these things. No one really wants to see me. I make the women nervous and the men don't want to look at old, lopsided Lana."

"Bullshit!" I said, "The men don't flock around you anymore because of your sour attitude. Relax, lighten up and they will still hit on you. I wish you would get it through your thick skull that you are still a sexy and desirable woman."

And she was. She had great legs and a fine ass, and with her new clothes and the padding she wore she looked great. It was just that she knew that they knew she only had one tit and that somehow lessened her in their eyes. Our sex life was still great and I fucked her every chance I got. I made her wear either garter belt and nylons or crotchless panty hose in case I wanted to pull over and fuck her in the car on the way home. She was always fine with me when we were alone. I was even able to joke with her about the missing tit. I'd tell her "at least now I don't have to feel guilty about not giving the other one equal time." But she just could not loosen up when we went out.

+++++++

After about a year I approached Charley, a very good friend of mine, and asked him for a favor. "I want you to make a pass at Lana at the next party we go to." He looked at me like I was crazy and I went on to explain everything to him.

"Hell, the only reason the guys don't flirt with her anymore is that she chases them away."

"I know that and you know that, so don't let her chase you away. See if you can break through her shell."

"Okay," he said, I'll see what I can do."

At the party that weekend I left Lana alone several times to give Charley a chance to flirt with her and I was pleased to see that he actually got her to laugh a couple of times. When we got home that night Lana was a wild woman in bed. I talked to a couple of other guys I knew and asked the same favor I'd asked Charley and they all agreed to give it a shot. Within six weeks Lana was back to being her old self. Guys were flirting with her at parties and she even got hit on a couple of times at the super market and mall and life was good again. I'd done my good deed and helped Lana get back her self-esteem and feel good about herself again.

+++++++

The good deed was done and the punishment for doing it was about to fall on my head. A good three months passed since Lana had mellowed out and one day I was out of the office to visit a client and I had to pass right by our house on the way back to work. I decided to stop and see if Lana wanted to have lunch with me. She wasn't home, but I noticed the message light blinking on the answering machine. I hit the play button and a voice I recognized said:

"Hey babe, we still on for this afternoon? If I don't hear from you I'll meet you at the usual place."

Now, I'd never ever had any reason to be suspicious of my wife, but there was something about that message that just screamed out "Hurry over here and fuck me." It was a Tuesday and Tuesday was the day Lana played bridge with some girlfriends. I went back to work and spent the rest of the day trying to convince myself that I was being foolish, but I could never quite get it done. I was almost home from work when I finally decided that I had to know, one way or the other. I pulled over and called home on my cell phone and told Lana that I had to work late. I parked one block over in front of our neighbor's backyard where I could look up his drive, through his backyard and into our drive and waited. Half an hour later Lana came out of the house, got in her car and drove off. I followed her halfway across town and watched her pull into the parking lot of the Starlight Motel and park. She got out of her car and went directly to one of the rooms on the ground floor near the end of the building. I waited until she was inside and then I walked the parking lot looking for what I knew I'd find. It was parked near the end of the building near the room Lana had gone into. I stared at it for several moments as I recalled a conversation I'd had several months ago.

"Don't let her chase you away," I'd said, "Break through her shell," and as I stared at the black Dodge pickup I realized that he had done just that. I took my cell phone out of my pocket and called the Starlight Motel.

"Mr. Halloran's room please."

A couple of clicks, two rings and then a voice said, "Hello." I broke the connection and thought, 'Charlie Halloran, you dirty rotten son of a bitch!' And then I remembered all the other guys I'd asked to do the same thing.

End of the 6th Story

Gloria and Staci

I'm broken hearted as only the young can be; deep despair, my life is over, oh woe is me. Gloria had been my girl since sixth grade. We were inseparable all the way through high school and into college. We started making our wedding plans in our second year even though we didn't plan on getting married until we graduated. I loved Glory more than life itself and then one night she broke a date with me because she said she needed to study for a test. Three hours later I was sitting with some friends at Hoagie's, a campus hangout, when I saw Glory come in the front door with a guy I'd never seen before. She didn't see me sitting in the back, but I saw her. I saw her kissing him in their booth. I saw her uptight against him out on the dance floor with both of his hands plastered on her ass, and I saw her when she ran her hand down the front of him to where his cock would be. I waited until they went back to their booth before I went over to them. She looked up when I approached and I saw her face lose some of its color. "Don't bother introducing me to your "study companion." I just wanted you to know that you're busted. Keep the ring. I don't want anything around to remind me of you." I turned to walk away and a hand grabbed my shoulder and a voice said, "You can't talk to her like that," and I turned and hit him so hard that he flew backwards into the booth, hit his head on the wall and just laid there. I gave Gloria the dirtiest look that I was capable of and then I turned and left.

For the rest of the spring term Gloria kept trying to call me, but I wouldn't talk to her. It was a little more difficult during summer vacation since she only lived four houses down the street from me. She kept trying to reach me, but I managed to avoid her. Her parents talked to my parents and I got all of the bullshit, "She didn't mean anything by it," and "You have been together too long to let a little squabble like this come between you," and other such nonsense. Gloria sent me letters and left me notes, all of which I threw away unread, and she even spent one entire day sitting on the hood of my car waiting for me to come out of the house. If I had been ten years older it might have been different, but I was young, my pride had taken a hell of a shot from the girl who was supposed to love me and there was no way in hell I was going to forgive her for what she had done.

+++++++

The one thing about being young though is that despair doesn't last very long. That fall I met Staci and she drove away whatever thoughts of Gloria that remained. I was mad about her and she seemed to feel the same way about me. She came home with me over Christmas break to meet my family and after a few days at my house we were going to go and see hers. My parents had a Christmas party while we were there and they of course invited Gloria's parents who of course brought Gloria with them. Gloria waited until I was in the middle of a crowded room and couldn't get away and then she came up and said, "Brian, we need to talk," in a loud enough voice to draw attention.

"I don't need to hear anything that you have to say. The last time we talked you lied to me and the last time I saw you were getting ready to cheat on me with another guy. I have nothing to say to you and you have nothing to say that I want to hear. Now go away and leave me alone."

I started to move away from her when her dad stepped in front of me. "You just accused my daughter of lying and cheating and I expect you to apologize to her right now."

'Okay,' I thought 'if you want this to happen in public, so be it.' "I will not apologize for telling the truth. If you don't like the way I have behaved towards your daughter since catching her with her hand on another man's cock, that's just too damned bad. But I did catch her and I am not going to forget it or forgive it. Now, get the fuck out of my way," and I pushed past him.

Of course my parents were horrified at my behavior at the party, but I told them that it was their own fault for inviting Gloria's parents knowing full well that they would bring her with them.

"It's the price you paid for meddling and trying to play match maker."

Staci wanted to know what it was all about and so I ended up having to tell her the whole story. She gave me a contemplative look and was quiet for a minute and then she said, "Can't blame her for being upset at losing you, baby. She knows she fucked up a good thing and she wants you back," and then she smiled, "But I'm not letting you get away so she is just plain shit out of luck."

+++++++

We went back to school after Christmas break and when spring break came, Staci went home to see her folks and I went home to see mine. Halfway through spring break I had an uncontrollable urge to see Staci and so I jumped in my car and made the four-hour drive to her parent's place. I turned on her street just in time to see her come running down the walk and jump in a car that was sitting at the curb. She slid over next to the driver and they kissed and it wasn't any little old peck on the cheek either. They held the kiss for almost a minute and then the car pulled away from the curb and I was just curious enough to follow. They drove to a roadside tavern and went inside and I gave them a couple of minutes and then I followed. Luckily the lighting was low except for around the band stand and dance floor and I was able to take a corner seat at the bar and watch them. Every time they danced the guy had his hands all over Staci and she did nothing to stop him. About two hours later I saw the guy call for the check and I went outside and got ready to follow them again, but all they did was start the car and drive back to a dark corner of the parking lot. I watched as they started necking and after about five minutes Staci disappeared from view and half a minute later I saw her legs come up. I guess I should have called ahead and let Staci know I was coming. An hour later I was behind them when the guy dropped Staci off in front of her parent's house. I drove to a 7-11 and called her and listened to her tell me how much she loved me, how much she missed me and how much she wished that I could be there with her.

"Well Staci, that's the problem. I am here. I turned onto your street just as you jumped in the car and gave the driver a pretty long kiss. I was at the tavern where I watched him do everything but fuck you on the dance floor and I was in the parking lot watching when he did fuck you in his car. I waited until you got home to make this call. Have a nice life," and I hung up.

For the rest of spring break Staci would call me four to five times a day but all I did was hang up on her. I avoided everyone else for the rest of spring break. I just wasn't very good company. What was it Yogi Bear said, "It was deja vu all over again?"

+++++++

The only reason I went back to school was to complete the last three classes that I needed to graduate. Staci kept trying to get me to talk to her and I kept avoiding her. She finally managed to catch me in a booth in a restaurant and slid in beside me so I couldn't get up and leave. She told me that she loved me, that she missed me, that she needed me and that the other guy meant nothing to her.

"I just used him for sex, baby."

She told me that she had a huge sexual appetite and that no one man could fill it. She told me that even though she had been dating me she had been seeing other guys on the side, but I was the one that she loved and wanted to be with. She begged me to understand and then she asked me to take her back and if I couldn't bring myself to marry her because of the way she was, at least stay with her and be her lover.

I sat there and listened to her talk about being mine while fucking other guys and then I said, "Were you not at my parent's home over Christmas when I had my little scene with Gloria? All she did was put her hand on a guy's cock on the dance floor and you saw how I behaved over that. You actually fucked another guy and I'm supposed to be okay with it? And now you say you want me to stay with you less than a minute after telling me that I can't satisfy you and telling me that all I would have to look forward to was life with a promiscuous slut? Fuck you, Staci! I should have stayed with Gloria."

She gave me a long look and then said, "Look, I love you. I can't help it. I love you and you are the man I want to spend my life with. There is more to a relationship than sex and I promise you that you won't lack for it along with all the love and devotion that I can give you. Please Brian, I don't want to lose you. Try and work with me on this. At least think about it, okay?" She leaned over and kissed me and then she got up and left.

I did think about it. I thought about what life would be like with a woman I could never satisfy and who I'd always know was out looking for another cock to get her hands on. No way I could see any future in that. I also spent some time wondering what it was about me that made the women I cared for go looking for other guys. I had put Gloria out of my mind so I should be able to do the same for Staci. Well, that wasn't really true. I still saw Gloria almost everyday around campus and every time I saw her I thought of all the good times we'd had and how much she had meant to me and then the image of her on the dance floor would come back to me. I guess I hadn't put her out of my mind, I'd just put her behind me and I'd just have to do the same for Staci.

I started dating again and I did meet, had fun with, and occasionally bed some very nice young ladies, but I never found one who could keep my interest the way Gloria and Staci had. Fine choice I had – one who was all set to fuck around on me and one who already had.

+++++++

I was sitting at a table in the cafeteria when Gloria sat down opposite me. I started to get up, "Please Brian, can I at least say I'm sorry and apologize for what I did?" I sat back down and said, "Okay, you are sorry, now leave."

I saw a tear start down her cheek and all of a sudden I felt like a heel. I don't know why I should have felt that way – after all, she was the one who had screwed things up – but still, I felt like a heel. "Okay, what is it that you want?"

"Just to talk to you, to try and explain why I did what I did. To try and make you understand that it had nothing to do with my feelings for you. I do love you Brian and I miss you terribly."

"Alright, go ahead. It probably won't change anything, but I'll listen."

When she started I almost slammed my book shut and left the table, "I did it for us, Brian. I did it to help our marriage."

As I said, I almost bolted, but then I became intrigued. How could her sneaking around with other guys behind my back be for us? It turned out that she had been reading one of Barbara Cortland type romance novels and it had occurred to her that she was in the same position that the woman in the novel had been in. The woman had grown up with and then married her childhood sweetheart without ever having dated another guy. She began to wonder what she had missed and what other men would have been like. She strayed, was eventually caught and her marriage was destroyed. She was devastated because she really loved her husband with all her heart while the men she had dallied with had meant nothing to her. The rest of the book was about her determined fight to regain her lost husband.

"I could see that happening to me, Brian. Even though I've never dated anyone but you, I've always been curious about other guys. I didn't want to get married and find myself wondering and then maybe during a rough spot in our marriage, deciding to find out what I had missed. I decided to sow my wild oats before we got married. But I love you Brian and I couldn't take a chance on losing you so I didn't come to you and tell you this. I was afraid that you would have turned your back on me and so I snuck around behind your back and managed to screw things up anyway."

"That night at the bar was the third time I dated another guy. The first two I didn't even like well enough to kiss goodnight, but I liked Steve, the one you hit, enough so that I was going to go to bed with him. I didn't though, because he got up and stormed out of the bar and left me there. I did get laid that night. I was hurt and upset and I sat there and drank and I let some guy pick me up. It was awful. Wham, bam and get out of my car bitch before you stain my seat covers."

"I tried to talk to you but you wouldn't even answer my calls. Then I got mad and went on a man binge. I had sex with at least eighteen different guys before I realized that I felt nothing for any of them and that everyone of them lacked the ability to make me feel the way you made me feel. Please Brian, give me another chance, please?"

I didn't know what to say. It sounded just stupid enough to be true. While I sat there and looked at her she waited for me to say something. When I didn't the tears started down her cheeks and she got up and started to walk away.

"Glory?" She turned to look at me, "Doing anything tonight?"

I showed up at her door expecting to take her out to dinner and maybe a movie. She met me wearing a bathrobe and told me to sit down and that she would be with me in a minute and then she left the room.

She came back two minutes later in nothing but high heels. She struck a pose and said, "I'm hungry Brian, but not for food."

It turned out to be a very long night for me and a very enlightening one. The lovers she'd had while away from me might not have made her feel the way she wanted to feel, but they had damn sure taught her a lot and I began thinking that there might be something to be said about sowing your wild oats. Glory was now teaching me what she had learned and by the end of the night I was debating sending her out to try another ten guys. She had always been lukewarm about sucking cock, but now she was a human vacuum cleaner. Before, she never would let me eat her pussy even when I begged, now she pushed her muff in my face and begged me to eat her. Before it had always been the missionary position and now she would do it hanging from the ceiling if she could.

As great as the sex was it had a downside – I was intimidated by it all. Her rationale for trying other guys, i.e., the fact that I was the only guy she had ever been withheld pretty much true for me. Until I broke up with her she had been the only girl I'd ever been with. Even considering the three months I'd been with Staci and the two or three I dated after her I was still pretty damned inexperienced. I felt like a babe in the woods when Glory finished with me.

It was nine in the morning when she turned to me and said, "Everything we did last night I've done with someone else. I want to do something with you that no one else has ever done to me. Something that will make me yours and that I will never do with anyone else (oh yes indeed, I caught that) – I want you to fuck me in my ass."

She went into the bathroom and came back with a jar of Vaseline and had me spend the next ten minutes using my fingers and my thumb to loosen her up and then she got up on the bed on her knees and put her head on a pillow.

"Go slow and easy, baby. You're going to hurt me at first, but it will get better."

It took me almost five minutes of going slow and easy before she stopped whimpering and started breathing hard and a couple of minutes after that she was crooning, "Oh yes, oh yes, oh yes."

I'd already cum so many times that night that I just couldn't get off in her ass and after twenty minutes we stopped.

"Next time we will do my ass first," she said, "I want to know what it feels like when you cum in my ass," and then she turned to look at me, "There will be a next time, won't there?"

I nodded my head and said, "How about tonight?"

She looked away from me and said, "I can't tonight baby, I have a date."

I stared at her for several seconds and then I said, "You try for months to get me to talk to you. You beg me to forgive you and take you back and when I take a step in that direction you say sorry, I have a date?"

She was silent for a moment or two and then she said, "You're right. I'll break it. I have you back now and that's all that matters."

I thought for a moment and then said, "Who is he and why was tonight important enough that you were going to say no to me?"

"Just a guy that I have been dating off and on for a month or so."

"You been fucking him?"

She looked down at the floor and said, "Yes."

"Were you going to fuck him tonight?"

"Yesterday the answer would have been yes. He's really good in bed and I would have brought him back here and fucked his brains out. Today's answer is no, I just thought that I should break it off with him but I wanted to do it in person."

I would not have believed it possible for me to go one hundred and eighty degrees in the space of ten hours, but I did. "Keep your date, but just remember – no one gets your ass but me."

She looked at me, absolutely stunned at what I had just said (it had kind of caught me by surprise too) and then she threw herself into my arms.

+++++++

We slept until noon and then we went out and had a big breakfast. As we ate we had a long discussion about our relationship – actually I did most of the talking and Gloria listened. We would 'kind of' go steady while having other relationships so that neither of us would feel like straying if we got married, and I placed heavy stress on the 'if.'

The only thing that Gloria said was "Are you sure about this? I don't want to do anything to drive you away now that I have you back."

I smiled at her, "Glory, be honest – you were going to keep on seeing other guys anyway."

She got indignant, "I was not!"

I laughed and said, "Glory, when you gave me your ass yesterday you said, and these are your exact words, 'Something that will make me yours and something that I will never do with anyone else.' That told me plain as day that you would be doing something with someone else, but that they wouldn't get your ass."

Her face flushed and she looked away from me. "Understand me on this Glory, sneaking around is what almost killed us. Whatever you do, you better be up front about it. I'll buy your story about getting it out of your system before you get married and I'll turn a blind eye on it as long as you are straight with me. But you better understand that I'm going to be out there getting a few things out of my system too. One last thing, remember your promise – your ass belongs only to me. Now, go get ready for your date tonight and have a good time."

That night my doorbell rang at two o'clock. I stumbled out of bed and went to the door and opened it to find Gloria standing there, "How do you feel about sloppy seconds?"

That night set the pattern for the next couple of weeks. Gloria would go out on a date and then come to my apartment to spend the rest of the night with me. Sometimes she had been fucked and sometimes she hadn't. I suggested that since she was spending so much time at my place that she give up her apartment and move in with me. But she said that she needed a place to take her dates if she decided that they were going to get lucky, "It would be too awkward to bring them here." So I gave her a key so she wouldn't have to beat on the door at two in the morning.

+++++++

About three weeks after Gloria and I started back together I was eating lunch in the school cafeteria and I had my head stuck in a book when someone sat down at the table with me. I looked up and saw Staci sitting there. "Hi," she said, "How have you been?"

"What do you want?"

"I see you have gotten over being mad at your old girlfriend. Does that mean there might be some hope for me?"

I shrugged, "Short-term maybe, long-term no."

"Why?"

"You have already told me that I'd have to share you for the rest of my life and I'm not willing to do that."

She gave me a surprised look and then she laughed. "You have to be kidding. You have to know that your little sweetie is fucking everything in pants. It's okay for her, but not for me?"

I explained to her the difference between what Gloria was doing now and what Staci would be doing for the rest of her life and she laughed at me again.

"Honey, get used to the fact that your sweetie will be fucking around on you for the rest of your life. Once a girl gets used to getting a lot of different cocks she will never be happy with just one."

She saw that I was going to tell her that she was wrong and she held up her hand to stop me, "I love you, Brian. I know that you don't believe that I can and still be the way I am, but I do. I want you all to myself, but if short-term is all I can get I'll take it and hope for the best. I've missed you lover. How about tonight?"

The next two weeks were among the most tiring of my young life. It seemed that every night I spent with Staci was a night that I would go back to my apartment and find Gloria waiting for me. I was in a position that most guys my age would have killed to be in – two gorgeous women who wanted to fuck me to death. The problem was that they were pretty damned close to doing it. My studies suffered, my grades started taking a nose dive and it seemed I started each day with less and less energy – Gloria and Staci had drained it all out of me. And then in a most unlikely way my salvation arrived.

Staci and I had gone to a party and then had returned to my apartment and we were in bed fucking up a storm. I was on my back and Staci was sliding up and down on my cock when I noticed Gloria standing in the doorway watching. Staci saw the look on my face and looked over her shoulder to see what I was looking at and I saw her grin. Then she surprised the hell out of me by saying, "Get your clothes off sweetie and join us." Then Gloria surprised me by starting to undress.

Staci stopped fucking me and asked Gloria if she had been fucked. The question took Gloria by surprise, but after a moment she nodded a yes. "Oh good," Staci said and took charge. "I love the taste of cum. I'll eat you while Brian finishes fucking me. Then we can take turns sucking his cock until he gets hard enough to fuck you. Between the two of us maybe we can keep him up all night. They did and it was an interesting and exhausting night. Staci sucked the cum out of Gloria, Gloria sucked my cum out of Staci, I ate both of them and they both sucked my cock and in between all of the above they fucked my brains out. I couldn't even make it to class the next day.

What happened that night was my salvation that didn't become apparent for another week. I had passed on a date with Staci and I was hitting the books hard for midterms. It was around ten in the evening and I heard a key in my door. I knew it was Gloria because she was the only one I'd given a key to. It was too early for her to be coming back from a date and so I figured that she was coming over to keep me company – wrong! It was Gloria alright, but she wasn't alone, she had Staci and three guys with her. She looked at me apologetically and said, "My place and Staci's place weren't big enough. You don't mind, do you?" Staci said, "Go ahead and study, lover. We will be waiting when you get done." Of course studying anything was out of the question with all the noise coming from the bedroom so I put my book down and went to see what was going on. One guy was fucking Gloria and Staci had one guy fucking her from behind while she sucked the cock of the third guy. Gloria saw me come in the room, "Hurry baby, it's not fair. She has two and I only have one. When the three guys left, Staci and Gloria went sixty-nine with each other and then the three of us fell asleep on the bed. I woke up the next morning not nearly as exhausted as was usual because of the help I'd gotten from the three guys.

It seemed that the girls had bonded the night that Gloria had walked in on Staci and me and they had started going out together. This was the third time that they had picked up guys, done them in the same room and then swapped partners. For the rest of the term the two of them hung out together. Maybe two nights a week they would bring their dates to my place, but the rest of the time they did their screwing someplace else so I could hit the books. The two of them would still come by my apartment almost every night, but by the time they got there they were pretty much fucked out and after I would do each of them once we would all fall asleep. My grades came back up and things got easier for me all around.

Gloria and I were married six months after graduation and Staci was the maid of honor. My bachelor party was unique in that there were two women who did a strip tease and then fucked everybody who wanted to fuck and as often as they wanted. It was also unique in that both women wore hoods so no one would know who they were. As a disguise Gloria and Staci also wore wedding rings so the guys (none of whom I'd gone to school with) would think that was the reason for the hoods. Things got a bit dicey when Gloria's brother showed up (uninvited) and was all set to take her from behind. I managed to get to Staci and whisper in her ear what was about to happen and she managed to intercept him and keep him occupied for the rest of the night. Later Gloria told me that I should have let him, "It would have been a kick and he would have never known."

Staci had known what she was talking about when she'd told me that once a girl got used to a lot of cocks she would never settle for staying with just one. Even though Gloria had said that once we were married she would stay on the straight and narrow, she couldn't do it. Just over a year after we were married she let my boss fuck her at the company Christmas party. She didn't hide it from me. She came up to me and told me that he had made a serious pass at her and that she wanted to let him fuck her. "Would you mind, honey? I've been a good girl for over a year now. Can I play, please?"

I told her to go ahead and he has been fucking her two or three times a week since then. He doesn't know that I know and it makes for some humorous moments in the office.

Staci came to visit about a month after Gloria started her affair with my boss and the two of them went out and partied. They ended up in a hotel room with six guys and didn't come home until noon the next day. Staci found a job here and will be moving in with us until she gets settled although both of them have indicated that Staci's taking up permanent residency with us is what they really want. I told Gloria that since she has my boss to play with I would sleep with Staci while she was with us and she said, "Bullshit! You can sleep in the middle."

I guess I can live with that.

The End

Here is a sample from another story you may enjoy:

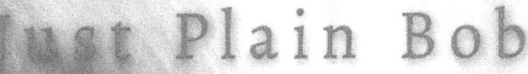

Just Plain Bob

7 INTENSE
STORIES IN 1

She
MAKES ME...

EROTICA SHORT STORIES, VOL. 16

What happened was Aimee. Aimee was the embodiment of the term 'California Beach Bunny'. Tall, tanned, long honey blond hair that hung to the middle of her back and a body built for the specific purpose of driving the male sex wild. Ted introduced us and then said, "Aimee and I are getting married."

Lucky bastard I thought even as I looked at her and thought that I had seen her someplace. You know how it is when you meet someone you think you've met before or seen some place? It crawls inside your head and stays with you as you drive yourself bananas trying to remember. She noticed my attention and she came over to me.

"Is there a sign on my back that says 'kick me' or are you staring at me because you are enthralled with my beauty?"

"Enthralled of course. That and the fact that I would swear on a stack of Bibles that I've seen you some place before now."

"When was the last time you were in California?"

"I've never been there."

"Well this is my first trip out of the state so I have no idea where we could have run across each other."

"Curious, but the feeling is there and it will eat on me until I resolve it, at least in my mind."

She shrugged and moved away to talk to somebody else and I went to find Teddy.

"Where are you staying while you are here?"

At the Best Western off Meadows and Founders Parkway."

"Bullshit bro. I'm sitting in an almost empty three-bedroom house and I could use the company. It gets lonely in that big place."

"Why don't you sell it? The place can't have much in the way of good memories for you."

"It is my revenge bro. The divorce decree gives Lisa half when I sell it, but not until I sell it and the decree doesn't set a time limit. If I live there for fifty years it means that cheating whore doesn't get a dime for fifty years. When we leave tonight we will swing by the Best Western and pick up your stuff. Tell Aimee not to worry. The house is so well built that it is almost sound proof. The two of you can raise all kinds of hell and I'll never hear a thing."

The party was running down and Ted and Aimee went to get

their coats and as we were heading for the door Aimee dropped her purse and bent down to pick it up. When she did her blouse rode up in the back and I saw the tattoo. It was intricate scrollwork about twelve inches long and maybe six inches high and as soon as I saw it the penny dropped and I knew where I had seen Aimee. I'd have to wait until I got home to make absolutely sure, but there really wasn't any doubt in my mind. When Aimee stood up she saw me looking at her and she read my facial expression and her facial expression told me what she saw – "He knows."

We made small talk on the way to the motel and then on the way to my house. Ted pointed out the local sites as we drove along, but Aimee was mostly quiet. She kept glancing over at me as if expecting that I would suddenly shout, "I know where it was that I saw you" and then proceed to tell Teddy. When we got to my place I showed them to their room and then I gave Aimee a tour of the place so she would know where to find things and then I bid them goodnight. I went to the living room and read until they had time to fall asleep and then I got up and headed for my home office. I booted up the computer, got on the Net and then logged onto one of my favorite sites. I went searching through the index until I found the section I was looking for, brought it up and there she was. Absolutely no doubt about it. The name on the clip was Lois, but it was sure enough Aimee.

I heard the door open and close behind me and I turned and saw Aimee standing there. "You know, don't you?"

I nodded a yes.

"All of it?"

Again I nodded a yes and pointed to the monitor where a clip from GangBang Squad was playing out. Aimee was on her knees inside a circle of five black men with large cocks and she was taking turns at sucking them. She looked over my shoulder, "I knew when I saw your face as we were leaving that you had figured it out. Not exactly my proudest moment."

"Maybe not, but you sure look good doing it."

"I was out of a job, the rent was due and I hadn't eaten in two days. I was really hurting for money when a guy I knew asked me if I would be interested in making fifteen hundred for something I usually did on weekend nights for free and I said yes. Only it wasn't like what I did on weekend nights. All I did then was pick out a cute guy and have some fun. I didn't know it was a bunch of black guys until I got there."

"Why didn't you leave?"

She shrugged, "I just said it. I was out of a job, the rent was due and I hadn't eaten in two days."

She pointed at the monitor, "You spend much time on that looking for porn?"

"Quite a bit. It is my sexual outlet since my wife left me for a couple of bikers."

"Then you will probably come across me again. After the gangbang I did a couple more to keep the money coming in until I could find a job. I did one for MILF Seekers, one for Her First Big Cock, one for Her First Anal and two for Suck Bus. You going to tell Teddy?"

"Of course not. He's happy, you seem happy, why should I screw things up for the two of you? I do have a question though."

"What?"

"I know how big Ted is in the cock department. You going to be happy with him in bed after all those huge cocks I've seen you take?"

"I won't lie. Big is good. Hell, big is great, but there is more to a marriage than just sex. Ted is very good in bed and as long as the love, affection, and caring are there what he has will be more than enough."

"Then I guess you should have a happy life because Ted has always given a hundred percent in everything that he does."

"Yes, well, I just have to make sure that he gets the chance to do it," she said as she moved toward me.

"What are you doing?"

"I'm not a very trusting person," she said as she took off her blouse.

If you enjoyed this sample then look for <u>She Makes Me</u>....

Also by this Author:

The Prodigal Family: The Abbotts

Watching My Shared Wife

The Waitress and the Runaway Husband

Baiting Mr. Little

Too Hot for Henry

Chuck's Fantasy

The Redhead's Desires

Rescued at Riley's

His Every Fantasy

Open Mike Night

Pursuit for Revenge

Why Does He Do That?

Halloween & Drugs

Tracey

When Rob Met Kari

Becoming a Shared Wife, Vol. 1 –

(Wife Sharing and Other Adventures)

Becoming a Shared Wife, Vol. 2 –

(Hazardous Wives)

Becoming a Shared Wife, Vol. 3 –

(Wives Who Stray)

Becoming a Shared Husband, Vol. 1 –

(Suck Me)

Becoming a Shared Husband, Vol. 2 –

(Husbands Who Stray)

Becoming a Shared Husband, Vol. 3 –

(Get even!)

Becoming a Shared Couple, Vol. 1 –

(Steamy Swingers)

Becoming a Shared Couple, Vol. 2 –

(The Share Thing)

Becoming a Shared Couple, Vol. 3 –

(Kathy is Wild)

Erotica Short Stories, Vol. 1 –

(Taboo Desires)

Erotica Short Stories, Vol. 2 –

(Nasty Steps)

Erotica Short Stories, Vol. 3 –

(Married But…)

Erotica Short Stories, Vol. 4 –

(Sizzling 10)

Erotica Short Stories, Vol. 5 –

(In My Wife's Panties)

Erotica Short Stories, Vol. 6 –

(Taboo Unlimited Desires)

Erotica Short Stories, Vol. 7 –

(XXX Stories)

From the Author

WANT FREE COPIES OF MY BOOKS?
Just visit my blog and download free copies of my books:
awesomeauthors.org/justplainbob

If you enjoyed any of my books then please share the love and promote my books in Amazon.

If you write me a review and send me an email I will send you a free book, or many.
(Just know that these emails are filtered by my publisher.)

Good news is always welcome.

One Last Thing, For Kindle Readers...

When you turn the page, Kindle will give you the opportunity to rate this book and share your thoughts on Facebook and Twitter. If you enjoyed my writings, would you please take a few seconds to let your friends know about it? Because... when they enjoy they will be grateful to you and so will I.

Thank You!

You may also like the books by these authors:

HIS WIFE *and* HER HUSBAND
SPOUSES WHO STRAY

HOT ROMANCE EROTICA
JACK RYDER

Shelly and I were always sort of mismatched now that I look back at the eight years we were husband and wife. I was always a night owl. Preferring the late night hours to write my stories when there were no distractions and the rest of the neighborhood was asleep.

Shelly was one of those early to rise and early to bed sorts. She spent her morning working out to keep her highly tuned body at its peak performance. She spent the rest of her day with her clients. Shelly was a very popular personal trainer in our little part of the world.

Things went fairly well the first three or four years of our relationship. We could laugh off our differences as amusing quirks that added to the uniqueness of our love. But after a while, those differences began to grate on us. It began to erode the foundation of that uniqueness.

Shelly was always so busy that she often left things a mess. It wasn't just a little mess either. She would leave any room she'd been in looking like a tornado had roared through. After years of cleaning up after her, I began to resent it. I felt like I was her personal maid or something.

It seemed that Shelly's biggest resentment was that I would try to get sexual with her when she was ready for bed. But she grew more and more resistant as the years went by. Often telling me she was too tired or that it pissed her off that I would get back up afterward to go do some more writing.

After a while, we fell into a routine of sorts. I stopped complaining about her messiness but became very quiet and uncommunicative when she was home. She responded by coming home later and later and curtailing our sex life to a holiday treat or as a favor when she wanted something special. Those episodes usually occurred each time I received a large bonus when one of my books did very well.

I'm sort of telling you all this boring stuff so you can get an idea of how we sort of drifted our own directions. I became accustomed to doing pretty much whatever I wanted to go do. And Shelly pretty much came and went as she pleased as well.

But you need to understand that I never once considered having an affair or seeking out companionship in any manner. I truly believed that we were just suffering through growing pains and that eventually things would straighten out for us.

I also have to tell you that I have a very active sexual drive. As time passed, I found ways to…take care of my own needs so to speak. I found ways to satisfy myself. I found there were many ways that one could have anonymous sex and there were many others that were seeking the same release.

It started out with a few harmless trips to the Adult Arcade out on the edge of town. The sign had just caught my eye one afternoon after having an argument with Shelly. She had taunted me afterward saying that the next time she would fuck me is when pigs fly.

I felt a little apprehensive when I first stepped into the arcade. Afraid I might see someone that I know and they would think I was some sort of pervert. I was surprised to see that there were nearly a dozen people milling around in the large center area that was filled with rows of videos, sex toys and sexy lingerie.

I noticed a couple of men over in the back corner by the gay magazine row. They seemed to be sizing me up as they gawked at the magazines they were holding. It even appeared that two of them were sort of petting each other below the level of the shelves.

There were a couple of middle age women that seemed like they were a little embarrassed to be here. But they were whispering requests at the counter clerk.

I figured they were here to purchase some stuff to spice up their sex life at home. I felt a little jealous as I thought of that. At least these women were trying to find ways to keep their sex life alive.

I also noticed one woman in the other back corner alone. She was holding up sexy panties as if inspecting them. But she kept looking over as if to see if I was paying attention to her. She was wearing a very short mini skirt and extremely tight pull over top. The way her nipples were poking against the tight cotton fabric, it was easy to tell she was not wearing a bra. She sort of looked like a hooker.

I noticed the hall way to the arcade with the private booths. I smiled at the woman one last time then made my way down the hall. I went to the very last booth at the far end of the hall and closed the door behind me. I quickly shoved $5 in the pay slot and selected a porn video to watch.

I just got my pants down and was gently tugging on my prick when I heard the door to the booth next to mine open and close. Moments later, I heard the sound of the machine taking money in the next booth. Then I heard a loud moaning as the porn came on in the next booth. In a few seconds, the sound became the same as the video that I was watching.

I was just getting a good rhythm to my jerking when I suddenly heard "Pssssst," coming from the wall next to me. When I glanced down, I saw a four inch hole in the wall at just the same level as my cock…

If you enjoyed this sample then look for **His Wife And Her Husband**.

LEE NORTH

Forgetting the Shared Wife

Erotic Romance

We were married in a small church in the suburbs that had time available the following April. I met Judy's family for the first time and I have to say, they were pretty cool toward me. I wondered why, but Judy dismissed my concerns. My folks were in good spirits and welcomed Judy to the family. But again, her parents didn't seem to warm to my folks either.

On the other hand, Judy seemed to be quite friendly with Mike. Perhaps because he was a professional athlete or maybe they just hit it off. At least it took some of the pressure off during the reception.

We went on a short honeymoon to Victoria and Seattle before coming home and settling down in our rented apartment. I was working hard to do well in my new sales job and so far, my boss was happy with my results. I had some objectives to reach this year and by mid-year, I was pretty sure I was going to achieve them.

Judy was happy to continue working in the lab. Her hours were more predictable than mine; seven-thirty am to four pm. Mine were irregular, often spending four or more hours on the road traveling from customer to customer, arriving home after six pm after battling heavy commuter traffic.

Life went along quite smoothly for us. We finally saved enough money to put a down payment on a townhouse in the suburbs and celebrated our third anniversary a week after we moved in. This would be our stepping-stone to a proper home someday in the future.

We talked about starting a family, but Judy was adamant that she didn't want to do that until we were more financially secure. She never was able to articulate just when that would be, but since we were both young, not yet twenty-five, there was no panic.

As with any marriage, things tended to slow down a bit in the sex department. Before we were married, we were having sex four or five times a week, except when she was having her period. That dropped to three times weekly after the first three years, and then as time went by, we were down to once or twice a week. When you're working as hard as I was, you don't notice these things right away, but after a while I did, and mentioned it to Judy.

"Judy, we don't seem to be making love as often as we used to. Is there any reason for that?" I started the conversation after supper one night when we were just sitting quietly on the back balcony of the townhouse.

"No. Why would there be?" The way she answered sounded strange to me. I suppose defensive, but a bit aggressive too.

"I don't know. We used to get together at least three times a week, but not lately."

"Well, we're both working hard and after all, you can't expect us to be full of energy every night." Again, I got that slightly aggressive tone.

"I suppose. But I do miss it. Making love to you is something I really enjoy." I was trying to make it sound inviting to her.

"You'll just have to get used to enjoying it a little less often for now. I'm not always in the mood, you know." I wasn't getting a very sympathetic hearing. I decided in the interests of peace that I wouldn't pursue the matter any further that night. But, it would get revisited.

If you enjoyed this sample then look for **Forgetting The Shared Wife.**

Amy Redek

Farell

Hot Romance Erotica

'It was a dark and stormy night and the lightening crashed and the thunder flashed,' I began before being interrupted by a bright seven-year-old girl.

'Excuse me, Mr. Farrell,' her right arm held up high, 'but shouldn't that be the lightning flashed and the thunder crashed?'

'Quite right, my young Miss. I changed the words to see if you were paying attention,' which proved that at least one was. This was becoming my party piece as I was always invited to the birthday parties of my niece and nephew and as the end of the party was nigh, I would always be asked to tell a ghost story. The floor would be cleared and we would only have the light of a solitary candle on the mantel piece behind me as the children sat in a semi-circle before me, holding hands. So in the gloom of the room with just this single flickering light that didn't show my features, I had to make the most of the story with the tones of my voice. They liked it when it was deep and sonorous to try and portray that somewhere outside of our circle was a mysterious and threatening presence. One year I didn't begin with those words and I had cries of dismay, so ever since, I've had to begin my stories the same way. They understood these words whether it be around an old house alone in the middle of the moors, or a castle perched high on a cliff edge with the seas crashing and rolling against the sharp jagged rocks that had seen many ships founder. They could imagine the single flashing light high up in the castle, luring a ship to its destruction on the rocks below.

These were pictures they could conjure up in their mind's eye as I described the wind and the way that it talks to man, bird and beast. This was the beginning to their story and it was not to be left out though the critics say that a book should never open with these lines, but it was the way that my critics who sat before me all wanted it to begin.

But my own story for you really started with it being quite the opposite, though if I ever got to tell it to the children, it would have to be different. Spring had arrived and the sun was shining and all seemed right with the world. My name is Michael Farrell and I'm slightly overweight for my height of six foot if taken with my being thirty two years of age. I have light blue eyes, clean shaven, average features and have brown to black coloured hair which is of no value to the story but just helps to fill up the picture for you to see me.

I live alone in a cottage, of which there are twelve in what is known as Meadows Lane that leads nowhere from the lane at the top. This top lane, or road is one of those nightmare thoroughfares that only has passing areas about two hundred yards apart. Not lay-bys but just bits of ground where the hedge has been crushed over the years and were now just bare patches of earth that were full of mud and icy water during the winter. Many's the time you can hear the honking of horns as two vehicles meet and neither want to reverse to clear the way. It is usually the one with a female inside that finally gives way and makes the tricky job of reversing round a blind bend to be able to pull into the hedge lined gap.

This was the road at the top of my lane and it had just a small pub and one shop that sold a lot of nothing, and to complete this part of the village, there were six cottages either side of these two public places. These were all on the right as we came out and turned left from Meadows Lane because the land opposite and onto which my cottage backed, was Meadows Farm.

It was over a quarter of a mile before we came to the stables on the right and this was directly opposite another lane that ran in the same direction as the one I lived in. Now this would show the ingenuity of the district's planning many years ago, because it bounded the other side of Meadows Farm and that my lane was called Meadows Lane, they named this one by just dropping the letter S. Brilliant thinking on someone's part. This lane too had twelve cottages and so it was almost a mirror image to mine if one could look down from above.

Now at the bottom of the two lanes and of the farm in between, was what were locally known as the cliffs. A misnomer if ever there was one like calling our hamlet a village. Our cliffs were about twenty foot high and as the land and soil slowly broke away with wind and rain, they became slopes that ran down to a narrow pebbled beach, if I could even call it that. Though the land of the farm was flat where the farmhouse stood, it rose up towards the sea end but rolled down on either side to where the lanes were, so from where I lived, I couldn't see the lane on the other side of these fields because of this small hill.

I know, I know, you're getting impatient for me to start the story but I had to give you the lay out and topography of the place first and you'll understand why in a minute. Now I'll get to the problem I caused our postie, postman to you townies, his name by the way is Pat. Well, that is what everybody calls him like they call our village Toy Town. We don't have a Noddy but we do have a Big Ears, but due to the size of the fellow, no one has ever dared call him that. Built like a brick…, er, outhouse, with arms and shoulders that many a tree would be proud to have limbs like that. He was much in demand at harvest time because he could pitch fork even the most soggiest of hay bales to toss it over twenty feet high onto the hay wagon.

But the problem I caused our postman was of my surname Farrell, because there was another man of that name in the opposite lane, only his Christian name was Nicholas. When we did eventually meet, it became Mick and Nick, mine coming first alphabetically. What compounded postman Pat's problem was none of the cottages had numbers or names and he delivered by the surname on the letter, so sometimes I got Nick's and he got mine if the writer dropped the letter S. Also I think Pat had an eye problem to tell the difference between the two letters of our Christian names.

It was a joke when it first happened as I got a letter that was meant for Nick and so I took a walk along the cliffs and over the hill to hand deliver it myself for which he opened a bottle of beer as a thank you. Then another day he delivered one to me and I reciprocated with a bottle of beer and a chat. Now this would happen three, maybe four times a year so we both now always kept a few bottles of beer available in the pantry as payment.

It was on this glorious spring morning that Pat delivered one for Nick to my cottage, so after I had my breakfast and washed up and put the things away decided to take over his letter. I put it in my jacket pocket and went out into the garden but stopped as I looked at the sorry state of my roses. I saw that they could do with a bit of nutrient about now if I wanted a good showing this year, so decided to call in at the stables first to order some manure.

I walked up my lane and turned left and gave a wave to Dave, the pub landlord as he was seeing to his weekly delivery by the draymen. I ambled along the lane, keeping one ear cocked for the sound of any approaching vehicle from either direction, but as we are such a way off the beaten track, we don't get that many. I called in at the stables and spoke to the head lad; lad? He was nearly double my age and agreed to drop a couple of bags off at my cottage though I stressed that only when there was time and not to rush, which was a bit of a joke because nobody rushed in Toy Town.

With the manure ordered, I then went down the lane to Nick's cottage and I called out as I entered the garden but only got silence as a response. I went round to his back door which was never locked and went in, calling out his name again. The kitchen was clean and tidy but still no Nick. I went and felt the tea cloth and found that it was damp which told me he'd eaten and washed up. I went to his pantry and took out a bottle of beer and put it in the middle of the table so that it was a reminder of what he owed me as I propped his letter up against it.

I went out closing the door and down through his garden for the walk along the cliffs back to my place. It certainly was a pleasure to walk through the grass and feel the first hint of warmth from the sun on my back so I took my jacket off and slung it over my shoulder, enjoying the slight breeze coming off the sea and I could hear what I thought were larks as I got near the top of the small hill.

It was by looking up into the sky and not looking where I was putting my feet that I tripped and went sprawling flat down on my stomach, and as I raised my head, came face to face with Nick. There, in the grass, eyes half closed and the mouth fixed in a rictus of a grin, a foot away from me was Nick's head…

If you enjoyed this sample then look for **Farell**.

Ben E. Dorm

Mrs. MOON

ROMANCE EROTICA

Conversation ceased when Mrs Moon entered. She paused and looked around, letting them see her as she gave the place the once over. It hadn't altered at all to her notice: ill-fitting, threadbare carpet, once blue but faded and dirtied by years of traffic, mostly scuffed and dirty work boots, all raggedy at the periphery and curled in one corner. The same old calendar hung on the wall, a bosomy young blonde smiling out, the young woman at least two years older than the year displayed in the calendar's header. A knackered settee sat against the back wall, while a remnant from some ancient kitchen stood in one corner, a freestanding unit brought in by someone to act as a surface upon which rested a kettle, a five litre bottle of water, and the makings for tea and coffee. There was a fridge next to the kitchen unit, unloved and unclean, its job being to keep milk cold during the working week as well as lager for the Friday afternoon drink-up. A low coffee table was in front of the sofa, much be-ringed by coffee and tea stains, an overflowing ashtray in its geographical centre despite the no-smoking sign on display.

"Hello, Mrs Moon," one of the men said, a stocky, grey-haired man, his hair cut very short to his scalp. The man pushed himself upright from where he'd been leaning against the fridge, his arms folding across his chest as he moved. Mrs Moon knew him to be in his late forties, the foreman of the workshop.

"Tim," she replied, acknowledging the greeting. She surveyed the assembled group, eying each in turn. "Hello, boys," she breathed.

Three of the four remaining men mumbled their hellos, the trio wearing the same garb as Tim, grease-stained, baggy overalls. They were ubiquitous twenty-something's, one of whom Mrs Moon found rather attractive. The other two were nondescript, longish dark hair in need of a trim. In Mrs Moon's eyes they were unremarkable in every way, except to serve as extra meat in Mrs Moon's diet. She couldn't even recall their names – Alan and Pete or some such. Anyway, she had no interest at all in their personal lives or their circumstances. The young mechanics were always changing, with one leaving to be replaced by another, Tim being a constant in all the months Mrs Moon had enjoyed her Thursday afternoon sojourn in their company. She nodded at the trio, two of whom were sitting in the questionable embrace of the sofa, knees high because of insubstantial support in the sway-backed piece of furniture, the good-looking one sitting on the seat of an old ladder-backed chair, his arms dangling over the back support, the chair reversed beneath him.

The fifth man, the one standing with his back to the rear wall, the man in the suit, she ignored completely.

"Are you ready?" Mrs Moon asked, moving into the room with an exaggerated swing of her hips. "I hope so," she added, facing square on to the sofa, fists on her hips. "Because I'm so fucking horny…"

If you enjoyed this sample then look for **Mrs. Moon.**

JOAN VEGAS

Hot Dates
Being Sandwiched
MFM AND RELATED ADVENTURES

HOT ROMANCE EROTICA

According to leading Sociologists, the number of American women who have opened their lives to intimate affairs has substantially increased in recent years. It is estimated that as many as 60% of all married women have had affairs. That's right... 60%! Yes, that's still less than the estimated 70% of all married men who are believed to have had affairs, but it reflects the fact that growing numbers of women are reaching out for sexual variety in their lives.

Sadly, traditional secret affairs still usually bring with them feelings of guilt and anxiety. Yet, it is understandable that women, just like men, want their sensual lives to be fuller, they want "newness," and they want the excitement of experiencing different partners and different sexual adventures.

I have always been a proponent of variety in sexuality for both men and women. But, I have advocated that couples share in the development of new pleasures for each other, that they intentionally allow each other to experience extra partner and that they actively participate in providing extra partners "as gifts" for their primary partner.

Some call what I advocate "open marriage." While I feel open marriages are far better than the traditional "closed," monogamous marriage, I feel that husbands and wives can enhance the open marriage concept by periodically inviting others to join THEM in bedroom play. I encourage couples to explore the addition of another guy or gal to their love play as a way to take an active role in providing their spouse with extra partners while doubling that spouse's sensual pleasures.

For decades (centuries?) men have talked to their wives about bringing an extra guy to their shared bed. Many men fantasize about watching their wife being serviced by one or more other guys. Sometimes it is the woman who proposes such a threesome (MFM - male/female/male, or female-centered threesomes). But, more often than not, the wife is the "hesitant" party, turned-on by the idea, but "hesitant" to really give it a try.

The following are comments gleaned from letters I have received over the last few years from women who have opened their lives to extra partners... not within the context of affairs, but within the context of threesomes or open marriage agreements. I will let them tell for themselves WHY they enjoy this way of expanding their feminine potential.

Joan

If you enjoyed this sample then look for **Hot Dates: Being Sandwiched**.

WANT FREE COPIES OF MY BOOKS?

Just visit my blog and download free copies of my books:

awesomeauthors.org/justplainbob